Going Gently

Books by Robert C.S. Downs

Peoples (1974)

Country Dying (1976)

White Mama (1980)

Living Together (1983)

CONFLUENCE PRESS / Lewiston, Idaho

Copyright © 1973, 1993 by Robert C.S. Downs.

All rights reserved.

First published in 1973 by Bobbs-Merrill Company, Inc.

First Confluence Press paperback edition 1993.

93 94 95 96 97 98   7 6 5 4 3 2 1

Library of Congress catalog card number 93-70627.
Printed in the United States of America.

ISBN: 1-881090-00-0

Publication of this book is made possible, in part, by the generosity of Lewis-Clark State College and grants from The Idaho Commission on the Arts, a state agency, and the National Endowment of the Arts in Washington, D.C., a federal agency.

Published by:

❷ Confluence Press, Inc.
Lewis-Clark State College
500 8th Avenue
Lewiston, ID 83501

Distributed to the trade by:

National Book Network
4720-A Boston Way
Lanham, Maryland 20706

For My Wife, Barbara

ONE

They came to the hospital on the same day, but at different times and in much different ways.

Mr. Flood arrived in the morning an hour and a half before his admission time, and all through the procedure he stood quietly next to his wife with his eyes bulging in fear. He was a short man, built square and compact like a thumb. There was the feeling one got about him that he had run his life in high gear, that at sixty-seven his energy was still so abundant that it might at any time turn upon him and devour him.

As he entered his room he motioned to his son to put the large suitcase on the end of the bed. Then Mr. Flood sat heavily in the straight chair next to the night table and put his face in his hands. His thin wife, whose drawn face sank sadly at the corners of her mouth, patted his head in a gesture that somehow stopped short, as if she were trying to tell him something with her hand but had forgotten what it was. Then, just as his son was saying his father was embarrassing him, the day orderly fishtailed around the corner of the room. He was efficiency barely contained in a gray hospital shirt. "Flood, B. Correct?" he said, and as all three Floods nodded he initialed a sheet on the clipboard he was holding. "Visiting hours are in the evening," he said. "You may come back then. Mr. Flood and I have things to do." With a flip of his hand he shot the yellow partitioning curtain along the side of the bed and sealed off Mr. Flood and himself. The orders came quickly: Undress; fill out possessions slip in top drawer of night table; put on hospital gown. "I got my blue pyjamas," Mr. Flood said.

"Put them with the rest of your things. They'll be checked," the orderly said. He slipped through the curtain at the end of the bed so quickly that Mr. Flood wondered for an instant if he had ever been there.

As he undressed in the small space the curtain billowed and jerked and he said, "Damn, damn," in quick, short breaths. Just as he finished and was getting into bed the orderly returned and opened the curtain. He looked at Mr. Flood, put his hands on his hips and said, "No, no, no. The thing's on backwards. The opening goes in the *back*." He reached out and while Mr. Flood sat hunched and lump-like the orderly positioned the gown correctly. "I don't suppose you've been in a hospital before," he said. Mr. Flood shook his head slowly. "Well, Mr. Flood, you've got a lot to learn."

Professor Austin Miller sneaked around the corner of the room a little after four that afternoon. He moved with a quick, unusual grace for a man of sixty-seven, and in his face there was pride in having gotten into the room without anyone's seeing him. When he was certain that no one had followed him down the hall, he turned and looked at Mr. Flood's sleeping form. "Old people," he said out loud, and then more to himself, "They always give me old people." He looked away in disgust and toward his bed by the window. As he approached it he unbuttoned his heavy old coat and took two bottles of whisky from the inside pockets. He put them

Going Gently

in the cabinet of the night table with great and loving care. When he finished undressing he snatched the possessions list from the night table and checked its familiar boxes. Then he piled his clothes neatly at the end of the bed, and just as he was pulling the sheet over his chest the orderly came in to prep Mr. Flood for surgery the following morning. When he saw Mr. Miller the little man made a U-turn so violent that it looked as if the prep tray in his hands would continue on a straight line of flight. Mr. Miller's face, an accidental arrangement of deep claw marks, composed itself into a smile of unusual warmth. He knew it would be almost instantly that he would confront the head nurse, Miss Scarli. He was right and he was ready. When she came around the corner of the door with her fists clenched as if she were holding two hand grenades, Mr. Miller said, "My dear Scarli, how very nice to see you."

"All right, Homer, how the hell did you do it?" Miss Scarli said.

"The east fire stairs," he answered softly, "and careful timing. Very careful timing."

"You know I've been waiting all day," she said.

"Of course you have, Scarli," Mr. Miller said. "And that's the precise reason your awesome efficiency breaks down. You never observe the obvious. Would you please have this gentleman fetch my ice water?" he said. He nodded directly at the orderly.

"This time, Homer," Miss Scarli said, "go easier on the drinking. I won't say anything so long as you confine it to the room. But no more parties on the sun porch."

"I can assure you I shall limit my consumption to an occasional highball," Mr. Miller said, and then he glanced at Mr. Flood again. "What's wrong with that bird?"

"None of your business," Miss Scarli said.

"I've been meaning to speak to you about my room assignments," Mr. Miller said, but Miss Scarli had already pivoted like a tank and was on her way out of the room. The orderly entered with the ice water and set the pitcher down with a gesture that showed his irritation. Mr. Miller went right at him. "You, young man. What's the matter with you?"

"I am now one hour and ten minutes overtime," he said, and turned to Mr. Flood.

"Well, so am I," Mr. Miller answered, and he poured out a portion of whisky that even for a much younger man would have been an entire cocktail party.

During their preoperative dinners the two men sat on the edges of their high hospital beds locked in a kind of elderly stare-down. Had they been dressed and not in a hospital, a first-class barroom brawl would have been a foregone conclusion. But they sat immobile, both only in gowns that barely covered their groins, their legs weak and veiny hanging down toward the floor. The color of Mr. Flood's face indicated he was fast approaching cardiac arrest, while Mr. Miller's eyes kept sweeping Mr. Flood's body as if he had just been offered a chance to buy it at a wholly reasonable price.

"So you're a salesman," Mr. Miller said with contempt.

"Only part-time," Mr. Flood answered slowly, feeling his way. "I'm semiretired."

"What do you sell?"

"It don't make no difference. If you want something moved, I'll move it. I've handled everything from notions to fiberglass speedboats."

"Bully for you," Mr. Miller said, and he poured some whisky into his cup of clear broth.

"You work?" Mr. Flood asked.

"No," came the controlled response. "Two years ago I was retired by the teaching profession to reflect upon thirty-seven years of largely repeating myself. Do you drink?"

"Doctor's orders," Mr. Flood said. He flashed a baby-soft palm in rejection.

There was a long pause between the two men while Mr. Flood mashed his saltines in his broth and Mr. Miller picked his cup from the tray and drank the mixture that was now at least ninety percent whisky. Finally, he said to Mr. Flood,

Going Gently

"And what do the wizards of the knife have in store for you?"

"I'm going to have an exploratory operation," Mr. Flood said.

"Fun."

"How do you know?" Mr. Flood said, his voice firmer.

Without a word, Mr. Miller dropped his gown to the waist to reveal two large crescent-shaped scars. One was dullish red and nearly healed. The other was a curled purple rope, the puckered suture wounds surrounding it like a perverse floral arrangement. "Tomorrow they are going to make it a triumvirate," he said. With visible effort he retied the gown at the back of his neck.

"Jesus damn," Mr. Flood blurted, his big eyes stuck to Mr. Miller's gown.

"I have cancer," Mr. Miller volunteered indifferently. He patiently watched Mr. Flood shift uncomfortably on the edge of his bed.

"You got it bad?" Mr. Flood said as if he were spitting out pebbles.

"I shall put it this way," Mr. Miller said, and he took his whisky glass and drank from it. "I have no intention of succumbing to cirrhosis."

"Jesus."

"I have, though, what you might call the good kind of cancer," Mr. Miller went right on, "if, that is, there's any such thing. I've been told it's slowly spreading from organ to organ." From the evenness of his voice it was obvious that he had said the same thing many times before. "Those signatures on my belly are from two abortive attempts to find my primary tumor. If they could get that, they say there's a chance they can radiate me. But I'm afraid it all comes down to the simple fact that I'm going to die."

"Say, now, you shouldn't go thinking that way," Mr. Flood said. "A guy like you got to be positive. You'll never get anywhere thinking like that."

"Shut up, Mr. Flood. You know nothing about it."

Going Gently

"What's wrong with you, anyhow?" Mr. Flood said directly, his eyes narrowing.

"I'm afraid I don't follow," Mr. Miller answered. He was surprised by the tone.

"You been on my back ever since you came in here."

"Obviously we cannot avoid our room assignments," Mr. Miller said.

"You're about the most rudest guy I ever met," Mr. Flood said flatly.

"Apparently you cannot distinguish between sarcasm and irony."

"That's just the kind of crap I'm talking about. Don't you ever say nothing right out, I mean without all that professor lingo?"

"If you find my mode of expression irritating, there's little I can do."

"Listen," Mr. Flood said, the anger sliding from his voice, "if we got to share this room, we got to try and get along."

"I have spoken this way for my entire adult life," Mr. Miller answered, "and I shall continue to do so for whatever is left of it."

"I don't care how a guy says something, it's what he's saying that counts," Mr. Flood said. "And I don't see nothing behind anything you say."

"And whose fault might that be?" Mr. Miller said.

"I don't know. Maybe the both of us."

Later in the evening, after the last visitor had left, the preparation for surgery began. The blood technician, the anesthesiologist, the resident to do his history and work-up, all followed one upon the other. They were familiar with Mr. Miller from his two previous operations, and they were cheerful and pleasant with him. Mr. Flood was all fear and resistance. He reacted to the taking of his blood as if he were being assaulted in an alley, and when the anesthesiologist asked him if any anesthesia had ever made him sick he stared up in infantile awe. Mr. Miller carefully observed Mr. Flood all during the various procedures, but he said nothing until Mr. Flood asked the resident how big the scar would be. "Stem to stern," Mr. Miller threw in, and he ran his finger from his throat to his groin. He watched with pleasure as Mr. Flood swallowed hard. The resident gave a short laugh and said to Mr. Flood that it wouldn't be bad at all. "When in hell are you going to find my primary tumor?" Mr. Miller said from his bed. "When you do my autopsy?"

"Professor . . . " the resident began patiently.

"Skip it, young man," Mr. Miller said, and he turned away.

When the resident finally left, Mr. Flood sat up in bed and turned toward Mr. Miller. "Something's bothering me," Mr. Flood said.

"So?"

"Nobody came to see you tonight," Mr. Flood said. He watched Mr. Miller open a book that looked far too large for his thin hands. "Why's that?"

"Because nobody came to see me."

"No family at all?"

"Did you get a red pill from the nurse?"

"Yes."

"Then why the hell aren't you asleep?"

"Can I have a drink?"

Mr. Miller slapped his book shut and got out of bed. He put his robe on slowly and took two glasses and the bottle of whisky and set them down next to Mr. Flood. Then, as he was positioning a chair beside the bed, he said, "Frightened?" He poured some whisky into the glasses. Mr. Flood's hand shook as he drank. "You had better take the pill now," Mr. Miller said.

"What the hell's really going to happen tomorrow?" Mr. Flood finally blurted.

"I'm not going to lie to you," Mr. Miller said.

"It's all right."

"They are going to carve you up like Sunday's roast," Mr. Miller said very quietly, almost talking to himself, "and when

Going Gently

you wake up tomorrow you're going to wish to God you were dead."

"A bitch, huh?" Mr. Flood said. His face was blank and dumb.

"Like nothing you ever felt."

"That's honest, all right," Mr. Flood said. He put his glass out for more whisky.

"You asked me," Mr. Miller said, "and I told you."

"I guess I better get some sleep," Mr. Flood said. He drank the whisky and set the glass down without looking up. Mr. Miller sat for a while and watched Mr. Flood turn his face to the wall and sink into a quiet sleep. Then Mr. Miller went back to bed to read and let the whisky have its effect.

Neither operation was successful. Mr. Miller's surgery was by far the more extensive, and several times during it the shallowness of his breathing and the irregularities of his heartbeat worried the surgeon. Still they cut and searched, but they did not find Mr. Miller's primary tumor, and after three hours they gave up. Mr. Flood's operation was short, and the surgeon had barely opened the peritoneum when he saw that Mr. Flood's insides were as filled with cancer as anyone who had ever had it and was still living. He did not even have to be deeply anesthetized, and in the recovery room he regained consciousness long before Mr. Miller. In his stupor he knew that his belly hurt, but he did not feel the deep, searing pain that Mr. Miller had predicted for him. He moved his head to look at a nurse, and when he heard himself ask, "How'd I do?" he thought he sounded drunk. Through her mask she told him he was all right now, and then he was swept down and away into a long, comfortable sleep.

The two men were wheeled back to the room by orderlies, and when the resident passed Miss Scarli's station he handed her the charts. "Both terminal," he said as if he were giving a weather report. "I give them seven, eight weeks. If that."

Miss Scarli walked with the stretchers to the room and helped put the men in their beds. Then she checked the intravenous apparatus, one in Mr. Flood and two in Mr. Miller, and as she leaned over Mr. Miller he muttered, "Scarli, did they get it?"

"You're going to be fine, Homer," she said.

"I hate you, Scarli, you godforsaken gorilla dyke," Mr. Miller said. She watched as his eyes rolled back in his head and sweat began to form in tiny glycerine balls along his cheekbones.

Then both men lay quietly, Mr. Flood's breathing long and cleansing, Mr. Miller's shallow, sometimes frantic. Miss Scarli stood for a moment looking at the two men, and she thought that the next seven or eight weeks would be hell on her. The orderly gave her the blood pressure cuff, and she quickly took two readings from Mr. Flood. She had difficulty getting accuracy on Mr. Miller, and it was not until she had the orderly pin Mr. Miller's arm to the bed that she was satisfied he was in no immediate danger. She repeated the procedure every fifteen minutes for several hours, and when Mr. Flood finally began to stir she withdrew the intravenous feeding and had the orderly take the bottle and its tall pole from the room.

"Mr. Flood," Miss Scarli said, "are you awake?" Her voice was like a lever under his head. "Mr. *Flood.*" At first he mumbled incoherently, but then he felt Miss Scarli's voice drag consciousness into his eyes. Miss Scarli watched as Mr. Flood raised the sheet and looked at his belly. "Am I bleeding?" he asked as he tried to identify the bright color of the merthiolate that had been used to sterilize his trunk. But before Miss Scarli could answer his head fell back and the sheet fluttered over his body in a long sigh. "Do you have pain?" Miss Scarli asked, again her voice pointed, direct. Mr. Flood rolled his head from side to side. "If you do, press the call button," she said. She took it from the night table, pinned the black
cord to the sheet, and placed the buzzer in his right hand.

"Son of a bitch," Mr. Miller hissed in a long, throaty whisper from his bed. "M.S., Scarli, for Christ's God's sake, M.S."

Going Gently

"I'm coming, Homer," she said. She finished smoothing Mr. Flood's sheet and then went to him.

"Remove these insidious needles from my arms, goddamn it. It'd be all right if you ran bourbon in the left one and water in the right."

"Thirty-two years nursing, Homer, and the first prize in regaining consciousness goes to you." She set about removing the needles.

"Your body's no good any more," he said. "You must weigh a hundred and seventy pounds."

"I'm too young for you, anyway," she said. She watched as the faint smile drained from his face. His cheeks first slackened, then hollowed, and for an instant they looked as if they were going to slide off their bones. His eyelids closed as if under a great weight. "Ride it out, Homer," she said, and she went for the morphine.

Toward the end of the afternoon both men were awake, and Mr. Miller looked over to Mr. Flood and said, "How are you?"

"It's beginning to hurt," he said.

"The first night is the worst," Mr. Miller said. "Christ, is it ever." His head flopped back to his chest.

"Why?"

"Because any minute," Mr. Miller began, and then he stopped while his mouth sucked in a short tube of air. "Because any minute they are going to come in and make you sit on the edge of the bed."

"I can't get up."

"I know, I know."

"I can't, I tell you."

"Then they will get you up," Mr. Miller said. Mr. Flood heard him suck air past his clenched teeth, and then he heard him try to shout, "M.S., Scarli." But his voice barely carried to door. Mr. Flood's thumb came down so hard on the call button that it would hurt him for the next two days. He pressed it as though he would pulverize it, and he kept on in a reflex manner even after Miss Scarli and the orderly had entered the room. She looked at Mr. Flood, who said, "It's him, he tried to call." It was then Miss Scarli saw that she had forgotten to secure Mr.Miller's call button. It hung straight down from its wall socket like a piece of bloated licorice. "I'm sorry, Homer," she said as she came toward him.

"Don't start blocking me just because they didn't get it," Mr. Miller said to her so quietly that only she heard. "I'm going to be around for a while, you know, and you're going to have to get control of yourself. Now let's have some M.S.—and a lot of it."

"After you sit up," she said.

"If it were hospital procedure, you'd make a dead man walk to the morgue," he said.

"You bet I would."

"All right," he said, "in a few minutes." His chest began to flutter in a series of short, recuperative breaths. Miss Scarli turned toward Mr. Flood. She took the three short steps toward his bed very slowly, almost as if she were afraid of him. "I can't, you know, I can't get up," he said. "Later on tonight, maybe, huh?" Miss Scarli leaned the bulky weight of her upper thighs against the side of the mattress and looked down at him. "I can't," Mr. Flood said again. His breathing shriveled into a shallow panting.

"Up," Miss Scarli said.

"No."

"Up."

"I can't."

"Get up, salesman," Mr. Miller whispered.

"Shut up, Homer," Miss Scarli shot at him without taking her eyes from Mr. Flood.

"I'm not going to. I can't," Mr. Flood said. His head began to flop from side to side.

"Peddler," came from Mr. Miller's bed, "look here." Both Miss Scarli and Mr. Flood turned their heads to see Mr. Miller straining into an upright position, his sticklike legs creeping out over the edge of the bed, his eyes glassy, distant.

"Do you see me?" he said through his teeth.

"Damn it, Homer," Miss Scarli said, lunging toward him. "You're going to rip." She tried to support him, but he protected himself from her with his left arm. Then she stepped back and she and Mr. Flood watched Mr. Miller finally jackknife his legs over the edge of the bed. Then he began to use his arms to raise his body, alternating them like a jack raising a car, until he was erect, his arms stretched out behind him like the legs on a sick chicken. "Do you see this, peddler?" His elbows shook like little birch twigs in a sea breeze, but he did not fall.

"All right, you proved your point," Miss Scarli said, "whatever it was." Mr. Flood had started to whimper very softly, his head flopping again, and he was saying, "I can't do it. No matter what, I can't do it." The orderly came in carrying the syringe of morphine.

"Give it to him," Mr. Miller said. "It's not going to do me much good now." Miss Scarli knew that he was right. She knew his pain was too far ahead now, that the morphine would work much too slowly to give Mr. Miller relief. Without a word she put the needle into Mr. Flood's upper arm, and she was surprised that he did not seem to notice it. Then she and the orderly eased Mr. Miller back down onto his bed.

"Scarli, I'm going to need a double," he said up to her, his breath coming in quick pants that barely went past his lips.

"What in hell did you go and do that for?" Miss Scarli asked.

"I don't know," Mr. Miller answered quietly, all of his strength gone. "Damn stupid, wasn't it?" He sighed and then added, "But it felt good. Just before I sat up when I knew I was going to make it."

Miss Scarli and the orderly turned to Mr. Flood. She rolled back one eyelid with her square thumb and looked at the pupil. "All right," she said to the orderly, and she flipped the sheet down away from Mr. Flood. The orderly inserted his hands into Mr. Flood's armpits, and Miss Scarli grunted once as she took his knees, bent them and then brought his chalky legs out over the edge of the bed. Mr. Flood's eyes popped

Going Gently

open like a doll's when he came into a sitting position. The orderly stood in front of him and held his shoulders while Miss Scarli tried to talk to him. "Mr. Flood, you are sitting up now. Look at me." Mr. Flood's head looked like a huge, turgid melon as it hung on his chest. With great effort he raised it slightly and looked at Miss Scarli. "I am sitting up," he slurred. "I don't want to be sitting up." His head fell back to his chest and the top of his body pitched forward slightly so that he leaned against the orderly like a contrite child.

For the next day and a half, consciousness was an elusive thing for both men. There were several brief periods when one would wake and take some fluids, glance at the other, and then, after a few moments of clarity, the pain would return and he would call for an injection.

Along toward midnight of the second day Mr. Flood was lying awake, and for the first time since he had been made to sit up he did not feel sharp pain. His breathing was slow and even, and his chest no longer tensed when he inhaled. When he reached for his water pitcher he found that he could extend his arm without causing discomfort. As he carefully picked the pitcher from the night table Mr. Miller's light went on and he saw him reach for the large book. "How you doing over there?" Mr. Flood asked softly.

"I couldn't accurately say without swearing," Mr. Miller answered. "Are you feeling any better?"

"Some," Mr. Flood said. "But I'm glad it's over."

"In a way it is a relief," Mr. Miller said.

"They got your thing, didn't they?"

"My elusive primary tumor? No, they didn't." Mr. Miller paused and then said, "The paradox of the situation, you see, is that they nearly killed me trying for it. I was not operated upon, I was excavated." From the position of his head he could not see Mr. Flood's face, which had just spontaneously emptied of what little color had come back to it in the last twelve hours. He supported himself on his right elbow and stared at Mr. Miller.

13

Going Gently

"But they will get it, won't they?" he said after a moment.

"No," Mr. Miller said, "but I knew they wouldn't. Somewhere way inside where the thing is, I knew they wouldn't." His tongue scraped along his dry upper lip.

"Sure they will," Mr. Flood said.

With what seemed like enormous effort Mr. Miller turned his head slightly and said, "I don't care about you, you understand that? Do you, peddler?" His head pivoted loosely back to his chest.

"A man's got to have some faith," Mr. Flood said, and there was a complacency in his voice that angered Mr. Miller.

"You stupid man," he said. "The only thing I have had faith in for the past five months is the act of my own death. You don't need faith to die, you need to respect the act. Do you hear that, peddler? Respect."

Mr. Flood eased himself back to the horizontal, and after a long silence he said to Mr. Miller, "I know they're going to get that thing of yours. Don't ask me how, I just know it."

The surgeon came in the next morning with Miss Scarli, and he motioned her to close Mr. Miller's curtain. She did so without looking at him. He lay flat and quiet, the rigidity of his body and the color of his face deathlike. He listened passively, the morphine oiling through him, as the surgeon and Miss Scarli registered their mutual approval of how well and evenly Mr. Flood's incision had come together. But when he heard the surgeon ask Miss Scarli to bring the chair over for him Mr. Miller's body gave a spastic jerk as he remembered involuntarily the same chair being pulled up to his bed five months before. "No," he said softly through his thin lips, and as the surgeon began to sentence Mr. Flood, Mr. Miller's lips silently formed the phrases and words as they tumbled like buckshot from the young doctor's mouth. Mr. Miller remembered every detail of his own ordeal, right down to the way the doctor's eyes had moved frantically in the beginning for a place to zero in on, and how they had finally settled on the pillow just to the side of his head.

"You have a very serious illness," the doctor said to Mr. Flood, and the same weak statement echoed through Mr. Miller's head.

"Half-ass Socratic questions now," Mr. Miller said to his feet.

"How serious is 'serious'?" Mr. Flood asked.

"What does 'serious' mean to you?" the doctor answered.

Then Mr. Miller knew that the doctor would now leave as soon as he could, that he would go out in the hall and light a cigarette and tell Miss Scarli how tough that had been on him. And when precisely that happened, Mr. Miller slid the curtain back so that he was able to see Mr. Flood, who was still staring at the straight chair where the doctor had been sitting. But when he saw Mr. Flood's wife and son come into the room he pulled the curtain back.

It was clear that Mrs. Flood had been crying long and hard, and the son looked as if he had spent the night before drinking heavily. His skin was a pale gray, the fluid in his eyes frozen solid. As Mrs. Flood began to speak the words caught somewhere around her rear molars and piled one upon the other until she simply gave up and submitted herself to the sob that jerked her body like a dying fish still on the line. Finally she sat in the chair and leaned her head on the edge of the bed as if it were an altar rail. Mr. Flood's son stood and looked at his father and then his eyes began to drain onto his cheeks. But no other part of his face moved. Then he said, "Oh, Daddy," very softly, more as an intimate sigh than a word.

"What's gotten into the two of you, anyway?" Mr. Flood suddenly barked.

"We know," his son said, nodding like a priest. "The doctor told us yesterday." They moved their heads forward, waiting for cues.

"Only thing I want to know is what kind of hospital they think they're running here," Mr. Flood said. He turned from his family to speak to the ceiling. "I don't know who the hell they think they're fooling around with," he went on. "You can't tell a man who's feeling fine he's got the flu, you know.

Going Gently

My bottom dollar says it's a computer that's messed things up." He paused and glanced at his family. "Sure, I just had an operation, but I know how I feel. Jesus damn, it's my skin I'm in, you know." His eyes popped open as he said, "What gets me maddest is they don't double-check these things before they go off half-cocked. You got any cigars, boy?" he tossed at his son.

"I'll get you a whole box," he said, and he started from the room.

"Just a five-pack," Mr. Flood said. "Cuts the wind." Then he turned to his wife and said, "I just want to see how long it takes these sons of bitches to come back and tell me who they mixed me up with."

"Remember the T.V. show we saw?" she said.

"Sure, same thing," he said.

"I mean, you feel pretty good, don't you?"

"Just a sore belly, Mother," he said. He patted his middle to show strength. "It won't take them more than a couple of hours, a day at the most, to straighten this thing out." Abruptly Mr. Flood's strength was gone, and he let his body relax. His wife rose from the chair and said, "You rest now. We'll be back tonight."

"Leave the cigars on the table," he said, and he went to sleep.

The following morning Mr. Flood felt a new strong energy come into his body, and when Miss Scarli came into the room he bellowed a good morning at her. "Any chance of seconds on the boiled egg?" he asked.

"None," she said, and she went to Mr. Miller's bed and drew the curtain back. "How're things?" she asked softly.

"Black," he answered. "Everywhere inside my head things seem black. I feel like I weigh three hundred pounds."

"Do you want some medication?"

"What do you offer for acute terminal depression?"

"You've got a standing order for M.S.," she said.

"Shooting me full of morphine would make it easier for

Going Gently

you," he said. "No, thanks. I'd rather my gut broiled away."

"Be realistic, Homer," she said.

"That's precisely my intention. I am not going to leave this pathos-strewn life with my soul mortgaged to morphine. I shall go out observing."

She nodded to him and turned to Mr. Flood. "You're looking better," she said.

"Fit as a fiddle," he said. "How's 'bout getting up today?"

"If you want," she said, "you may sit in the chair for twenty minutes."

"Let's go," he said, and he began to raise himself up. But when he finally dropped his legs over the bed he got very dizzy. He thought he had concealed it well until he heard Miss Scarli say, "Not so damn fast." She got his robe from the closet and put it around his shoulders. Then she bent down and eased the paper slippers onto his feet. "When you stand, do it slowly," she instructed. Mr. Flood moved off the bed and stood for a moment, his body looking like a question mark. He took two short breaths and then held himself erect. Instantly he started to pitch toward the easy chair at the foot of Mr. Miller's bed. Miss Scarli steadied him. He moved, waddling, as though his trunk would get him there without his legs. "You're overweight, you know," Miss Scarli said to him. She supported him as she would a much older man.

When he was finally seated he let his body relax against the back of the chair. He asked Miss Scarli for a cigar and she handed him the pack. He took one out, slipped the cellophane from around it, and smelled it. Then he held it between the first two fingers of his hand and tapped the end of Mr. Miller's bed. "How you doing there?"

"A little more dead," Mr. Miller answered from behind the curtain.

"You hear about me? About how they got me mixed up with some other guy?" Mr. Miller did not answer. "I guess you been conked, huh? Well, yesterday they told me I'm supposed to have some sort of serious illness. That's more or less what the guy said. Jack E. Asses, that's what I say. You can't go tell

17

somebody who's walking down the street feeling A-O.K. that he ain't going to make it through the next block. Hell's bells, all they went and done was to mix me up with some other guy." He tapped the end of the bed again. "What do you think of that?"

"I think," Mr. Miller said from behind the curtain, "that you're wasting valuable time."

"How you mean?"

"They told you that yesterday," Mr. Miller said.

"So?"

"And now it is today."

"It'll take them a while to straighten things out," Mr. Flood said. He sniffed at his cigar again. "You know what's for lunch?"

"No."

"Croquettes, chicken croquettes."

"Detestable," Mr. Miller said. "In fact, I hate everything connected with this butcher shop."

"Why, this is one of the best hospitals . . ."

"*Fact*: This hospital has twice within the last four years been threatened with accreditation loss."

"They've got some of the best doctors," Mr. Flood said. "Everyone knows that."

"Everyone wants to know that," Mr. Miller said.

"Then why the hell aren't you down in Boston at the Mass. General or some place?" Mr. Flood asked. His hand tapped the bed harder.

"To hell with that," came the answer. "Too many experts."

"Maybe you're not going to like this," Mr. Flood said, "but couldn't you use you some experts?"

"Perhaps in theology," Mr. Miller answered.

Miss Scarli came through the doors with the young resident behind her. She said, "Twenty minutes, Mr. Flood."

"Well, Doctor, I see you've come with the good news," Mr. Flood said.

"How's that?" the doctor said.

Going Gently

"Come on, now," Mr. Flood said, his face rounding into a genuine smile, "quit the kidding, huh?"

"Scarli," Mr. Miller ordered, "do my curtain." She snapped it away from the end of the bed and Mr. Miller raised himself up slightly to look at the doctor. "Young man," Mr. Miller said to him, "tell my friend here that you've discovered your error."

"Gentlemen, really," the doctor said. "I don't follow at all." He glanced at Miss Scarli, who turned away and fumbled with Mr. Miller's curtain.

"Sure, fun's fun," Mr. Flood said, "and a good laugh's a good laugh, right?"

"Right," the doctor said.

"Get on with it, then," Mr. Miller said.

"With what?"

"With telling me who you've got me mixed up with, that's what," Mr. Flood said.

"Indeed," Mr. Miller added. Mr. Flood looked at him and nodded.

"There seems to be some mistake," the doctor mumbled, looking quickly from the men to Miss Scarli. This time she turned to pick up a water pitcher.

"Of course there's been a mistake," Mr. Miller said. "All you have to do, young man, is own up to it. Tell my friend here whom you have mistaken him for."

"There's been no error to my knowledge," the doctor said.

"Say, now," Mr. Flood said. He shoved the cigar into his mouth and bit down on it. "What the hell's going on now?"

"I told you this was a fourth-rate establishment," Mr. Miller said to Mr. Flood.

"I'm beginning to get the drift, I'll tell you that," Mr. Flood said. He snatched the cigar from his mouth and held it in the air like a small telephone pole. Then he quickly put it back between his teeth.

"Was this hospital your first choice for a residency?" Mr. Miller said to the doctor, and when the young man hesitated Mr. Miller pressed him hard. "Well, was it?"

Going Gently

"Not exactly," the doctor said.
"What number was it?"
"Ninth," came the quiet answer.
"Which means, of course, that there are eight luckier hospitals somewhere," Mr. Miller said.
"I'd like to know if you're really a doctor, you know," Mr. Flood said. Then, to Mr. Miller, "Lots of fakes walking around these days."
"And your internship?" Mr. Miller said. Color, good color, was in his face now.
"In a government hospital," the doctor said.
"Salvation becomes increasingly elusive," Mr. Miller said.
"And where did you intern for the government?"
"An Indian reservation," the doctor said.
"Then you are a doctor with a social conscience," Mr. Miller said.
"I would like to think so," the young man answered.
"Well, I wouldn't, sonny," Mr. Miller said.
"Now you look here," the doctor said. He gripped the stethoscope and yanked it from around his neck.
"Show me a man with a social conscience," Mr. Miller said, "and I'll show you one lacking a moral conscience. Now tell my friend here how you went and fractionated his reality." Mr. Miller lay back on the bed completely satisfied.
"You were an Indian doctor?" Mr. Flood said, just then catching up to the conversation.
"Indians are people, you know," the doctor said, relieved that Mr. Miller was out of the conversation.
"Not to me," Mr. Flood said. "Now you get the hell on out of this room and don't never come in here again." The resident looked at Miss Scarli, and when she started for the door he turned as if he were on a leash and followed her. "I'll be glad to get out of this place," Mr. Flood threw after them.

At dinner that evening Mr. Flood was given his first full meal of solid food. He sat on the edge of his bed and ate well. Mr. Miller was still much too weak either to take solid foods

Going Gently

or to sit up unaided. The orderly had slid his bed table almost directly under his chin, and Mr. Flood watched as Mr. Miller paddled a teaspoon through a bowl of chicken broth. He took a spoonful and tried to bridge the distance between the bowl and his mouth, but his hand shook too much and he spilled the liquid on his neck. "God damn it," he said slowly. He wiped his throat with the bedsheet.

"Take it easy," Mr. Flood said. "Getting your strength back takes time."

"Which is precisely what I haven't got," Mr. Miller said. "I knew I shouldn't have let them excavate this time. It's going to take so bloody long to get back on my feet. I've got things to do."

"I'll be going home in a few days," Mr. Flood said. He put a well-done square of lamb chop in his mouth. "Is there anything I can do for you?"

"Jerk."

"There you go again," Mr. Flood said, and he carefully balanced a cluster of peas on his fork. He put them in his mouth and said, "But I'm beginning to figure you out, you know. You ain't really mad at me. You're mad at everything. Don't get me wrong, I would be too, all things considered."

"Suppose I told you I *was* mad at you? The world, too, but you in particular?" Mr. Miller said.

"I wouldn't believe you," Mr. Flood said. Then he added, "Damn tough lamb."

"And why not?"

"No reason for it. You got a raw deal and you're mad at everything that walks in front of you. Can't blame you, though."

"Jerk."

Mr. Flood began a low, guttural chuckle and then froze in mid-laugh as his severed abdominal muscles started to contract. The pain forced a mashed pea from between his lips. Mr. Miller watched as Mr. Flood's face flushed and his eyes watered heavily. "Not completely healed yet, eh, Superman?" Mr. Miller said.

Going Gently

When Mr. Flood finally recovered control he looked to Mr. Miller and said, "You are a mean son of a bitch."

It was at that moment that the evening nurse, Mrs. Marvin, came into the room. She was a very small woman, and her general appearance suggested that she had been successfully resisting mandatory retirement for a good number of years. Age had completely flattened her chest and ballooned her ankles. Her nurse's cap, which looked like a sketch for a steeple, leaned off the right side of her head as if it were giving directions. "Swearing? Did I hear swearing from you?" she threw at Mr. Flood.

"I am afraid so," Mr. Miller answered for him. "Brought up in the gutter." He rolled his head away in mock disgust.

"I run a clean and proper floor," Mrs. Marvin said. "Do you hear that, Mr.—er—what is your name there?"

"Alfonso Gustavo Medici," Mr. Miller answered again.

"You had better be quiet, Professor," Mrs. Marvin said. Then, "Oh, yes, Flood, isn't it?"

"Yes, ma'am," Mr. Flood said softly.

"Swearing does not usually go unpunished while I am in charge," she said.

"Deny his bedpan privileges," Mr. Miller said.

"Do you want an injection tonight?" she said directly to Mr. Miller.

"It's quite possible that I shall require one," he said, but he knew that he had gone much too far, and that if he did not give in to her she would keep his medication from him as she had done on two previous occasions.

She turned back to Mr. Flood and said, "Your wife is here to see you and she's forty minutes early. I can let her in now or I can make her wait, you know."

"I'm very sorry," Mr. Flood said.

"Well, then, that's a good deal better," she said and she turned and left the room.

Mr. Flood raised the knife in his right hand as though to throw it, and he glanced at Mr. Miller just as he was about to shout. Mr. Miller had his forefinger on his lips and he was

Going Gently

gesturing to Mr. Flood to maintain silence. He knew that Mrs. Marvin was standing just outside the door listening.

Mrs. Flood came into the room like a fundamentalist on the way to heaven. There was a slight upward tilt to the chin, a squaring of the shoulders, a feeling about her that said enormous pleasure lies in denial. She nodded to Mr. Miller and then pulled the straight chair up beside her husband's bed. She placed a large shopping bag next to the chair and then leaned over to kiss Mr. Flood. She went for his forehead, but she stopped a fraction of an inch short and kissed the air with a dry, popping sound. Then she sat down and began to unbutton her coat. "How are you, Mother?" Mr. Flood said.

"About as well as can be expected," she answered. She put the coat over the back of the chair so that the torn lining about the armpits was clearly visible. "You don't know what a mess the house has gotten into," she said. "Gale never in his life has picked a sock from the floor."

"Where is he?" Mr. Flood asked.

"Why, it's Thursday," she said to him. He nodded in comprehension that his son worked late on Thursdays. Then there was a silence between them and they looked at each other. Mrs. Flood was the first to break the long, embarrassing moment. "Have you seen a doctor today?" she asked.

"Have we," Mr. Flood said with delight, and he turned slightly to look at Mr. Miller. "I think you could say we destroyed a doctor today. Isn't that right, Mr. Miller?"

"I daresay," he answered. Then he reached up and turned out the light and Mr. Flood looked back to his wife.

"Did Gale get his third-quarter taxes in?" he asked.

"I don't know," she answered.

"Now you tell him he's got one more year to average," he said.

"He knows that," Mrs. Flood said.

"He's smart, all right."

Mrs. Flood reached down into the shopping bag and took out a long black album. She set it across her lap

and folded her hands on it. "You remember this?" she said.
He looked at it for a moment and then his forehead creased and his eyebrows pulled together in concentration. She picked it up and turned it so that he could read the faded goldleaf lettering: GLADYS and BERNARD, JULY 17, 1939. "I'll be dinged," Mr. Flood said. "Where in hecks did you find that?"

"I've kept it in the linen closet," she said. She opened it like a Gutenberg and let her hand feel its way across the first page. Then she rose and set the album down on Mr. Flood's bed and leaned her spare hipbone against the edge of the mattress. She started to turn the pages slowly and to talk as if she had been rehearsing the words for months. Names, dates, dress colors, flower arrangements, songs, anecdotes, all dribbled from her mouth in a soft, sure rhythm. She went from black and white photographs with faded, obscure faces to color pictures which looked as if they had been fried. She had something specific to say about each, and she took little notice when her husband stumbled over an occasional question. "And remember when we finally left the reception and you couldn't start the car?" she said. She pointed to a photograph of a squat two-seater Ford.

"I forgot the keys, didn't I?" he said.

"They were in your other trousers," she answered, "in the suitcase in the rumbleseat."

"That's right," he said. He smiled faintly.

"And this is us driving away with all the shoes tied to the back fender." She turned the page with a little snap of her wrist. "You remember the Lovelys," she said. "Jack and Margot?"

"No," he answered softly.

"She sent the Christmas card last year with the note about John?" Mr. Flood looked at the group photograph in which all the faces were indistinguishable. "You know he finally passed on."

"When?"

"I don't know. I'm going to write her this week."

It was then that a wave of intense pain rolled up Mr. Flood's

Going Gently

trunk and smacked hard into his cheekbones. "Jesus," he said, and for a moment his wife chatted on. She stopped and asked if anything was wrong when he pushed the album away and slid down onto his back. "Jesus," he said, "I hurt like crazy."

"You shouldn't," she said. "They told me there wouldn't be much pain."

"Get the nurse," Mr. Flood said.

"You shouldn't be having pain," she persisted.

"Please."

"It'll be all right in a moment," she said. She opened the album again and began to describe the photographs they had taken on their honeymoon. "Bathing suits then certainly were something," she said. "I was using all that padding. I'm almost ashamed of myself. And look at how thin you were." Mr. Flood was gripping the sheet with both hands. "And there're those wonderful White Mountains way off in the distance."

"Please, the nurse," Mr. Flood hissed.

"If you want," she said, and she turned toward the call button. "You're sure, now?" she asked, and when he said please again she pressed the button and turned back to the album. "Now what was the name of those people who had the next cabin over from ours?" she said. "Here they are in the canoe. Johnson, Johnston, something like that, wasn't it?" She went on, her mouth a jukebox of memories, and she ignored her husband, whose head was moving slowly from side to side. When Mrs. Marvin came into the room Mrs. Flood stepped back from the bed and pressed the album to her chest. Mrs. Marvin came over to Mr. Flood and said, "You want a shot?"

His head stopped wagging on the pillow and he said, "Why's it hurt so much?"

"Don't know," she said. "These things do, sometimes, that's all," and she turned and left the room.

Mrs. Flood had her nose in the album as though it were a bestseller. "Mother," Mr. Flood said, "I'm sorry for not paying any attention."

"It's all right," she said without looking up.

"It really does hurt," he said.
"If you say so," she answered. "Johnstone, that's their name. I wonder what ever happened to them. From Illinois, never been East before. You remember she thought she was pregnant right off, just like that?" Mr. Flood's head started wagging again, and it did not stop until a few minutes after Mrs. Marvin had given him the injection. His wife continued to sit in the chair, the album in her arms like a baby.
"Is he asleep?" Mr. Miller said after a few moments.
"Yes," Mrs. Flood said. She turned sideways to look at Mr. Miller. He put his light on.
"I couldn't help overhearing," he said. "You seem to have such a splendid collection there." He nodded to the album.
"Why, thank you," she said.
"My wife's dead, you know," he said.
"I'm so sorry," Mrs. Flood said. She turned more toward him.
"For many years now I've lived all alone."
"Has it been hard?"
"Sometimes at night," he said. "You know what I mean?"
"Yes, I certainly do," she said. "When you can't sleep and you think the night's never going to end. When Bernie's been on long trips," she said, "well, the loneliness is just so ugly."
"Even sleeping pills don't help," he said.
"I know only too well," she said. She folded her arms tightly about the album.
"You must have some wonderful memories there," he said. She hugged the album closer. "Oh, I do," she said.
"Would you show me some of the photos?" he asked.
"I'd love to," she said, and she rose straight up out of her chair and went to Mr. Miller's side. She put the album down across his middle and he tilted it up to look at the pages. He went through the book carefully, mumbling interest, and occasionally he openly approved of a particular pose or group of people.
"I think I hear your husband stirring," Mr. Miller said.

Going Gently

"I didn't hear anything," Mrs. Flood answered. "This is one of us after our six-mile hike."

At that moment the orderly came into the room on his evening rounds with the fruit juices and ginger ale. "Tomato juice," Mr. Miller said. "Extra large."

"I thought you didn't like tomato juice," the orderly said.

"Nonsense, I love it," he answered.

The orderly poured out a large glass of juice and handed it to Mr. Miller.

"Do you know what this man wants?" the orderly said.

"He's asleep," Mrs. Flood answered.

"I could leave him something."

"Well, then, orange juice," she said. She stepped away from Mr. Miller's bed and accepted a small glass of orange juice and set it down on her husband's night table. While her back was turned, Mr. Miller poured the tomato juice over the album. "Oh, damn," he said, "I've spilled everything." He had done an expert job of ruining the album. He had closed the book and had poured the juice down through the top so that all the pages were covered. "*No!*" Mrs. Flood shouted. she snatched the book from him and whirled away from the bed. A thin line of tomato juice squirted from the bottom and laced itself in little dots across Mr. Miller's face and along the wall. "I'm terribly sorry," he said. He wiped a bubble of juice from his cheek and tasted it. "Awful stuff," he mumbled.

"You've ruined it, you've ruined it all!" Mrs. Flood shouted. Mr. Miller reached up and pressed his call button. "Damn you all to hell," she said. "That's the whole trouble with you all. You don't care about anything but yourselves."

"Nothing could be more accurate, Mrs. Flood," Mr. Miller said. Mrs. Marvin entered the room and Mr. Miller said to her, "This woman needs an injection. Hysterical broad."

"See what he did, see this?" Mrs. Flood said. She held up the album.

Mrs. Marvin put a bony arm around her and said, "Come now, we'll go out to the lounge and clean ourselves up."

Going Gently

As she led Mrs. Flood from the room Mr. Miller heard her say, "My husband was always so clumsy that way."

Mr. Miller awakened very early the next morning, and from the way he lay in bed his first observation was the purple streaking in the long sky out the window. From the light in the sky he knew the exact time, and he knew it would be well over an hour before the night staff went off duty. He lay immobile, his old, small body seemingly molded into the mattress, and for a moment he thought that he would never be able to move the great weight of his legs. He was relieved when he heard a sound in the room, and he turned slowly in the bed to see Mr. Flood standing halfway into the closet. "Good morning," he said.

"Not me," he heard Mr. Flood muffle into the closet. "Where the hell'd they put them?"

"Put what?" Mr. Miller asked.

Mr. Flood popped his head out of the closet and looked at Mr. Miller as if he had just uttered a gross obscenity. "Why, my *clothes*," he said.

"What do you want them for?"

"You're dumber than I thought you were."

"What do you want them for?"

"I'm getting me out of this here booby hatch," he said. He looked back into the empty closet. "Not me," he said.

"Yes, you, peddler," Mr. Miller said quietly.

Mr. Flood's body gave a small jerk and his back hunched slightly. For a moment his head stayed in the closet, and then very slowly he backed up and turned to Mr. Miller. "What do you think it is?" he asked.

"I don't know," Mr. Miller said.

"Look, what the hell *is* a serious illness?"

"That's what you have to ask," Mr. Miller said. "When you're ready."

Mr. Flood shuffled over to his night table and took a cigar from the pack. "Want one?" he said, and he held the pack up.

"No," Mr. Miller said, and then, as Mr. Flood set the pack down, "Well, why the hell not? Yes, I'll take one." Mr. Flood handed him the pack then offered a match. "Not right now," Mr. Miller said. Mr. Flood lighted his cigar and asked Mr. Miller for the time. "I should say six-fifteen or so," Mr. Miller said. "I stopped wearing a watch a long time back."

"Why?"

"I was always looking at it. Drove me half out of my mind. I'd have days when I'd simply look at the watch and stay looking at it until I had watched an entire hour go by. That, I believe, is what one calls desperation."

But Mr. Flood was slowly tuning out Mr. Miller. He had shuffled past the foot of Mr. Miller's bed, and for the first time since he had come to the hospital he looked out of the window. What he saw was a fat, gray fall morning shoving its roundness toward the small industrial town. All the yellows and reds of the New England autumn were gone into small whirlpools of screen-thin leaves and naked little stems. Even the ocean, a sliver of which was visible just beyond the town's two smokestacks, looked grime-covered and uneasy. Mr. Flood took a long puff on his cigar and stood for a moment in the bleak clouds. Then he waved his hand slowly and the smoke, on command, dispersed.

"What's it doing out?" Mr. Miller asked.

"Nothing," Mr. Flood said quietly, "nothing at all."

"Won't be long before snow," Mr. Miller said.

"I hate the goddamn winter," Mr. Flood said.

"It seems like the older you get . . . "

"I should have gone to Arizona when I had the chance," Mr. Flood said.

"So should we all."

"There ought to be a deadline, you know," Mr. Flood said, his breath on the windowpanes, "some kind of time when they come to you and say, 'that's enough, you deserve a good long rest in a warm place.'"

When Mr. Miller did not receive a breakfast tray, he knew

Going Gently

that he had been scheduled for one series of tests or another. When Miss Scarli and the orderly wheeled a stretcher into the room shortly after nine Mr. Miller helped them as best he could to get on it. As they started from the room, Miss Scarli said, "You know where you're going?"

"I couldn't care less," Mr. Miller answered. "It's only a part of the continuing plot to keep yourselves busy."

Mr. Miller was returned to the room over two hours later. He was much too weak and tired from the G.I. series to notice that Mr. Flood had pulled himself into a grossly exaggerated fetal position, and that his body was shaking as if intensely cold. They put Mr. Miller into his bed and left the room without so much as a glance at Mr. Flood. After a while Mr. Flood rolled over and, still in his tight ball, said, "What did they do to you?"

"X-rayed the gut," he said. "They make you drink a barium-hemlock mixture and then they X-ray, X-ray all the while shoving the hell out of your sore belly."

"I asked them," Mr. Flood said quietly, almost privately.

"And?"

"Not good."

"Never is."

"What am I going to do?"

"Bitch and moan like all the rest of us," Mr. Miller said.

"How much time you got?"

"They didn't tell me," Mr. Miller answered, "but my estimate is six, perhaps seven weeks."

"They told me six," Mr. Flood said. He rolled onto his back and cried out, "No, it's got to be longer. I got to have more time."

"It could be five weeks," Mr. Miller said. "Maybe four."

Mr. Flood did not hear him. He was mumbling, "Why me, why me?"

"Why any of us, would be more appropriate," Mr. Miller said.

Going Gently

"But I never did nothing in my whole life to have this happen," Mr. Flood said.

"No one did," Mr. Miller answered.

"Why me?"

"Everybody thinks that when he gets it it's going to be quick, splendid, and with just a dab of heroism. No one ever thinks he's going to be nibbled away."

"Why me?"

"Mr. Flood," Mr. Miller said, "have you ever been so angry at something in your life that your brain seared, that your entire body was ready to explode?"

"I never done nothing to anybody," Mr. Flood said. "I've always been a good guy."

"You might expect that to end," Mr. Miller said. "And you might expect that soon you will be so angry that you will not even recognize yourself."

"I'm going to be good," Mr. Flood said.

"If you are, I shall be very put out with you."

"I want to see Glad," Mr. Flood said.

"Well, you can't. The only people Scarli lets in outside of visiting hours are the old Catholic priest and the undertaker."

"Oh, God," Mr. Flood moaned, and it was a true, pitiable moan, "I don't want to die. Not in six weeks I don't want to die."

"Then when is a good time? I shall put in an order for you."

"Why in God's name are you so mean to me?" Mr. Flood said, his voice whining. "I never done nothing to you."

"Because there is so damn much to do you wouldn't believe it."

TWO

Three days later, in the early afternoon, the orderly came into the room and asked Mr. Flood if he wanted a shave. Mr. Flood was lying on his bed with his bathrobe on. He told the orderly that he was able to do his own face, but he knew that Mr. Miller was still too weak. "You want a shave?" the orderly said. He woke Mr. Miller from a light sleep.

"How very thoughtful," Mr. Miller said.

"Miss Scarli said you hadn't been shaved in three, four days."

"I wonder why Scarli is suddenly so concerned with my beard," Mr. Miller said.

The orderly set about pouring the hot water into the little steel basin, and then he lathered Mr. Miller's face. As he shaved the skin he saw that the soap came away from Mr. Miller's face, but none of the beard. He bore down, cutting Mr. Miller along the cheekbone, but Mr. Miller said nothing to him. "Sorry," the orderly said. Finally, when Mr. Miller's cheek had been cut in seven places, the orderly opened the

Going Gently

razor and looked at the blade. It was so rusted that the brand name was illegible, and the edges of it were caked with old soap and long hairs. "This the prep razor," he said, and he turned and left the room.

"One can only imagine the places that razor has seen," Mr. Miller said. Then, to Mr. Flood, "Do you have a styptic pencil?"

"I use an electric razor," Mr. Flood said.

"May I?" Mr. Miller said, and Mr. Flood took it from the bottom of his night table. When the orderly returned Mr. Miller had completed shaving himself except for his neck, and as the orderly watched he tilted his chin up and ran the razor over the rough surfaces near his Adam's apple. Then he unplugged the machine from its cord and handed both to the orderly. "I didn't mean to do that," the orderly said.

With considerable effort Mr. Miller turned toward the night table. He opened the top drawer and took out a five-dollar bill. "Here," he said to the orderly, "I want you to get me a bottle of whisky."

"What kind?"

"It makes no difference," Mr. Miller said. "The kind that gets you drunk, I suppose. And keep the change for a new razor blade." The orderly scooped the basin, soap and razor into his arms and left.

"You still got a bottle and a half," Mr. Flood said. "You expecting company?"

"Very amusing," Mr. Miller said. "No, I am not expecting company. But I think this evening I shall go calling."

Later in the afternoon the orderly brought the whisky to the room, and Mr. Miller asked him to bring a wheelchair before he went off duty.

And going calling was exactly what Mr. Miller did. Just after the evening orderly brought the juices around (Mr. Miller took a large glass of apple juice because, he said, it was the color of whisky) he struggled into his bathrobe, a dark blue rayon one with torn lapels. Then he had Mr. Flood slide the wheelchair to him and he got in it. He took the fresh bottle

Going Gently

of whisky and opened it. He poured half the apple juice into a bedpan on the straight chair and said, "Nobody'll know the difference." He filled the glass with whisky. He put the bottle in the right corner of the wheelchair behind his hip and then sipped from the glass. "A bit tart," he said, and his body shuddered slightly.

"You don't look like you ought to be up," Mr. Flood said after carefully observing Mr. Miller's ashen color.

"Strength is a state of mind," came the answer.

"You ought to get a pill and go back to bed," Mr. Flood cautioned.

"Why don't you go knock down a wall?" Mr. Miller said. Then he added, "If that sadistic Marvin bitch comes in here, don't do anything but play dumb. Tell her you don't know where I am. Tell her you've been asleep or something."

"I think you're crazy."

"That's the first smart thing you've said." And with that Mr. Miller cradled the glass in his crotch and wheeled himself from the room.

Mr. Miller was not gone long before Mrs. Marvin found him. He went up the hall to the next room, where he talked with a young man who had broken his leg in nine places in a motorcycle accident. Mr. Miller told him that it served him right, and then he gave him three-quarters of a glass of whisky and they talked about how long the young man would be in the cast.

As Mr. Miller was leaving the room he stopped his wheelchair at the foot of the bed by the door. He leaned over as far as he could and looked under the bed. When he saw the drainage bottle with its thick rubber tube snaking up and around the edge of the bed he shook his head in revulsion. Then he wheeled himself into the hall and very nearly into Mrs. Marvin.

"Well?" she said.

"My dear Mrs. Marvin," he said.

Going Gently

"None of that," she threw at him. "What were you doing in there?"

"Nothing," he said. "I merely cut the man's catheter, shut off his oxygen supply and benevolently administered Extreme Unction."

"No injection for you tonight," she said.

"I am above pain," he said, and he turned the chair sharply and wheeled himself back to his room.

He found Mr. Flood huddled again on his bed, his face to the wall. Mr. Miller turned his chair to look at Mr. Flood, and he drank some whisky. "It'll come and go," he said. "Getting used to it is worse than the thing itself. You were just sitting there feeling numb, or you were lying back with nothing particular on your mind." Mr. Flood had stopped his trembling, and although he was still turned away, Mr. Miller knew he was listening. "It is an ugly black wave that sweeps out of the ugly nowhere and grabs that life essence in you and just plain strangles it." He watched Mr. Flood nod slightly. "It's the kind of feeling you can't even stay with, let alone get ahead of," Mr. Miller said. He took some whisky. "How's your belly?"

"It hurts some," Mr. Flood said. "but what I can't stand is the way I'm feeling about everything."

"Like you haven't got the strength to move—ever," Mr. Miller said. "Like you could just lie there and go on out without ever moving or seeing or talking." He sipped again.

"What is it?" Mr. Flood said.

"Fear."

"I don't feel afraid," Mr. Flood said.

"And depression. But mostly fear."

"What did you do about it?" Mr. Flood said. He was still with his face to the wall.

"*Did?* It's hardly in my distant past," he answered. "When it comes I know damn well I can't do anything but let it run its course. If I can get a pill or a shot, I take that. If not, I drink." He raised his glass to toast the air.

"Do you think it'd be all right if I had a drink?"

"Get yourself an injection," he said. "There's no hangover."

Mr. Flood rolled over slowly in bed and pressed his call button. Then he looked at Mr. Miller and said, "Why have you been doing all this?"

Mr. Miller looked at him squarely for a moment and then said, "Because I need you." Then he abruptly turned his chair and, with an energy reinforced by the whisky, wheeled himself into the hall. He looked to the left to see if Mrs. Marvin was coming, and when he saw the hall still empty he pivoted the chair and wheeled himself rapidly in the other direction.

The following morning Mr. Flood summed up Mr. Miller's appearance when he said, "Jesus, you look like hell. Lot of pain in the night?"

"When I told you to get an injection last evening, I didn't know what you'd be missing," he said. His face was chalky and sunken, but there was a spark, a plain vitality to it. "I discovered that this floor is at full occupancy," he said, "and that's the reason Marvin couldn't get her hands on me last night. At least for a while she couldn't. And I'll tell you the floor's a frightful mess," he went on. "Fair group of drinkers, though." He looked to the nearly empty bottle of whisky that stood like a sentinel on his night table.

"How many people on this floor?" Mr. Flood asked.

"*Patients*, not people," Mr. Miller said. Then he added, "Fourteen not counting us. And by and large it's a messy group. I counted two prostectomies, one leg fracture in nine places, a bilateral mastectomy, two kids waiting to have their tonsils yanked this morning, and—let's see . . . " He bit into a dry piece of toast. "One cardiac fellow made to lie perfectly horizontal and restricted booze-wise, one colostomy, two disc people in the same room who hate each other but have made up under the influence, as 'twere, three executives with simple hernias, and one very seductive young thing in a blue transparent nightgown who, unfortunately, is afflicted with nine severely ingrown toenails." Mr. Flood chuckled with his mouth full of scrambled eggs. "And nine of them had at least

Going Gently

a shot from my bottle," Mr. Miller said with evident pride. "Several of them even wanted to buy it from me," he went on. "I could have gotten eight dollars for half the bottle. And I should have. Inside of half an hour everyone was sailing along as high as you please, and Marvin was half out of her mind with all the call buttons going a mile a minute." He stopped to catch his breath and nibble again at the toast. "I was about a room ahead of her, and I think I would have made it back here just fine except she double-crossed me and instead of answering the call in room twelve she just keep going on down the hall and, well, there I was."

"What'd she do?"

"Swore," Mr. Miller said. "For the first time in her professional life she swore, 'My God,' she whooped, 'the whole damn floor is loaded.'" He chuckled to himself, and then he added, "She brought me back here and I drank myself to sleep."

He looked at the empty sentinel again. "What do you think she'll do to you?" Mr. Flood asked.

"Nothing," Mr. Miller answered, "absolutely nothing. They wouldn't dare." He pushed his tray away and eased back on the bed with great care. When he finally let himself relax he took several deep breaths and said, "How'd you make out last night?"

"The shot did the trick," Mr. Flood said. "I woke up a couple of times, but I wasn't so low."

"It's marvelous the way depression just goes away by itself," Mr. Miller said. "Like a robber after he's used his blackjack."

Two days later Mr. Flood did the following: When the night nurse took his morning temperature she woke him from a sound sleep, jabbed the thermometer against his lips, and finally wiggled it into his mouth, hitting his front teeth in the process. Mr. Flood fell asleep on his side and when he awakened forty minutes later the thermometer was still in his mouth. He snatched the instrument from his mouth and threw it with as much force as he could against the open door of the room. It ricocheted into the hall, where it shattered into a spray of fine, sharp grains. It was not long before Miss Scarli came into the room, and as soon as Mr. Flood saw her he said, "If that ever happens to me again I'll do more than throw the damn thing."

"I realize the error, Mr. Flood," she said, "but night staff is hard to come by."

A few minutes later, after the breakfast trays had been given out, Mr. Flood sat on his bed and felt an anger roll through him that frightened him. He could feel it start near his incision and whirl and boil down into depths he did not know he possessed. He picked a knife from the breakfast tray and put on his robe, pushed the tray onto the floor and left the room. He walked the length of the hall to the sun porch, stopping at its doors to read a sign that hung from the doorknobs: "Not for patient use." He snatched the sign away and went inside. He was stunned a little at first because the place was very cold. Then his eyes began to pick over the room, going slowly from article to article, all the while his control over his anger like a tourniquet on a severed artery. Then, spontaneously, he tried to destroy the place. The first thing he did was to hurl the knife at the windows at the far end of the room. It went through a small pane with no noticeable deflection in its line of flight. He turned then and took a small wicker stool and threw it at the light. It broke the bowl and the bulb inside of it, and when it came down it bounced back and hit him sharply on the shin. He drop-kicked it fifteen feet to the other side of the room, where it took down two pots that sat gray and empty on a cantilevered bookshelf. Next came the flimsy coffee table that sat in the middle of the room. He gripped the legs at one end and simply snapped them off. One leg he put, like an expert knife thrower, halfway through the back of a large wicker chair. The other banged harmlessly along the floor toward a far corner of the room where it whirled out its force in a stationary spin. He was reaching for the other two legs when his strength gave out. It was a spontaneous draining from his body: Anger, strength, determination, energy all

Going Gently

vacated his frame simultaneously, and he had to stagger to the couch to avoid an outright fall. He sat for a moment, his mind nothing but a great white sparkling illusion. He stared at the doors to the room, but he did not react when he saw Miss Scarli and two orderlies come in. The only thing that registered in his mind was that they were afraid of him, and in his morphine haze on the way back to his room that fact pleased him enormously.

He awakened just after noon, and he found that they had put up sides on his bed and that a strap lay across his chest. When he put his hand on it he was faintly disappointed that it was not fastened. The orderly brought the lunch trays into the room, and when he saw that Mr. Flood was awake he went immediately for Miss Scarli. Before she could get to the room Mr. Flood was able to reach out and shove the lunch tray onto the floor. Miss Scarli never said a word to Mr. Flood. She gave him another injection, and she fastened the strap across his chest and pulled it very tight.

All the while Mr. Miller sat on his bed and stirred his vegetable soup.

When Mr. Flood awakened in the late afternoon, he found Mr. Miller sitting in the easy chair at the foot of the bed reading. Mr. Miller looked up over the rims of his glasses and said, "They think you've gone loony."

Mr. Flood put a hand on the guard rail and said, "Jesus, I feel awful."

"Exercise like that is debilitating," Mr. Miller said.

"Why'd they do this to me?" Mr. Flood asked. His hand moved a few inches along the rail.

"It was either that or shipping you to the state people down the coast," he answered. "They think you're section eight. Important conferences all afternoon, debates over tranquilizers to try on you. Everything but the problem, of course."

"They aren't going to send me away, are they?" Mr. Flood asked.

"Don't know," Mr. Miller said. "It was taking the knife

Going Gently

that bothered them most. Lethal qualities and all that, don't you know."

"I wasn't going to do anything with it," Mr. Flood said.

"I know that," Mr. Miller answered. He let the book lean gently against his chest as he took off his glasses. "I tried to tell them what was wrong with you, but they were having none of me."

"What'd you say?"

"I told them you were mad," Mr. Miller said. "No pun intended. Just outright mad. Then this intern, who looked rather like he had not yet been admitted to secondary school, began to charm the others with a sophistry or two about 'spontaneous paranoid schizophrenia.'"

"I don't know what that is," Mr. Flood said, "but I ain't got it."

"I know that," Mr. Miller said. He held the glasses by the stem and slowly twirled them. Then he said slowly and deliberately, "How do you feel?"

"Cleaned out," Mr. Flood said. "Very good and tired. I feel a kind of softness all over."

"Relief," Mr. Miller said.

There was a long moment between them while Mr. Flood looked at the ceiling and Mr. Miller cleaned his glasses with the end of the bedsheet. Finally, without taking his eyes down, Mr. Flood said, "What'd you do when you found out?"

"I was a good deal luckier," he said as if he were picking up a year-old conversation. "It didn't happen to me until I got back to my flat. I was terribly weak—you're weaker at home than you think you'll be—and the only initial statement I was capable of was the heaving, one by one, of twenty-three brandy glasses into the fireplace. With, I might add, the delight that comes from premeditation." He saw Mr. Flood smile. "Then, about ten days or so later," he went on, "I was out one evening on my first real walk and, my heavens, it was a beautiful evening. There was a sunset I shall never forget. The air gentle and soft like warm pillows." He was losing

Going Gently

himself in the memory. "I had taken the same walk many times, following the back streets down by the shoreline where all the sailboats and summer yachts sit like paintings while the sun on its way down bleeds into the water." He no longer heard his own words. "I was just there alone and seemingly not alone while all the gulls and sandpipers first dined and then lazily rolled out toward the point and settled down in among their rocks." Mr. Flood had rolled his head toward Mr. Miller and was watching him intently. "Then the sun with an enormous heave and groan started to grind itself unmercifully against the horizon, into the stinking black line of it, and it shot its redness along the water toward me like a giant universal hand. Then the sky went dull, intellectualizing itself away from me, and then there was nothing there any longer."

"Where'd you learn to talk like that?" Mr. Flood said softly. "I never heard words go like that."

Mr. Miller looked up at him, and for a moment his face was an open passage into his soul. Then it began to close down and he said, "I read too much." He put his glasses back on and picked the book from his chest. He stared into it for a moment and then said, "Oh, yes. On the way back to my flat I broke the radio antenna from every car I passed. I think there were eleven."

Mrs. Flood's first words that night, after she wiggled out of her coat, were, "Forty-eight fifty a day, did you know that?"

"What is, Mother?" Mr. Flood answered.

"It'd be sixty-seven-something if you were in a private," she went on.

"It's pretty reasonable," he said, "What with things nowadays."

She moved her hand in the depths of a large purse as if she were trying for a goldfish. "And the bill from the surgeon came, too," she said. Her hand came up empty. "It's some place," she said.

"Steep?"

"Seven *hundred*," she said. "Seven hundred and fifty dollars."

"That's not so bad," he answered.

"For who?"

"All things considered."

"Maybe all right for you, but multiply forty-eight fifty over six weeks or so and you've got a pretty penny. I figured it out," she went on, "and do you know what it's going to cost?" She answered her own question. "Almost three thousand."

"It can't be helped," he said.

"What I want to know is how I'm going to pay it."

"We've got the savings," he said. "It's near eighteen thousand."

"Somehow it's very unfair," she said.

"There's the three hundred a month," he said. "It's a good base."

Mrs. Flood rose slowly and said, "I have to be going. I promised Gale a late supper when he gets home. It's inventory week, you know."

She took her coat from the back of the chair, and as she did so she began to cry softly.

"What's the matter?" Mr. Flood said.

"I don't understand," she said, and she began to move toward the door with the timing of an actress going to a footmark. The tears were running free now.

"What don't you understand?" Mr. Flood asked, bewildered.

"I don't understand why you're doing this to me," she said, and with perfect timing she was gone from the room.

"Ah, families," Mr. Miller said.

"What'd I do?" Mr. Flood said, his bewilderment compounded by his wife's departure.

"Your mistake is that you're dying," Mr. Miller said.

"She's mad at me, isn't she?"

"You're not much good at understatement," Mr. Miller said.

"Why's she so mad?"

"Because you're dying."

"I need her."

"And she you."

"What's wrong?"

"Distance," Mr. Miller said, "the simple distance between us all."

"That's no help."

"I know that. But you'd better get used to it."

"She wasn't here more than ten minutes."

"I'm surprised she came at all."

"She's got no right to be mad at me."

"Yes, she does," Mr. Miller said. "You don't meet her needs."

"I'm getting sick of you," Mr. Flood shot across the room. "You're always in some goddamn book and you've always got every answer. It's so easy for you, you ain't got nobody."

"I never said that," Mr. Miller answered softly. "I have a son and a daughter."

"Well, Mr. Know-it-all, where are they?"

"My daughter is in Ohio in a convent, and my son is vegetating somewhere on the West Coast."

"They know about you?"

"I wrote to my daughter last summer and told her that I have cancer and she promptly replied that she'd pray for me and perform the necessary acts of penance and humiliation for the salvation of my everlasting soul."

"Is she coming to see you?"

"Hardly. You see, she is a member of the society of Christian Masochists: No talking, no reading, just kneeling. Been in the same cell praying for everlasting souls for over twenty years now. I don't even know her any more."

"But your son," Mr. Flood said, his anger swept from him.

"The letter I got from his platoon leader—it's here somewhere in my things—said he took a bullet in the head, left side I recall, on a hillside north of Seoul. Only problem is that he didn't die. When they flew him back to the army hospital I went out to see him, but he was just glassy-eyed and floppy-armed." He paused for a moment and Mr. Flood watched him as his gaze moved along the wall as if he were following a cockroach. "I don't know where he is now, they've moved him from place to place so many times."

"I'm sorry," Mr. Flood said.

"Be anything but sorry," Mr. Miller answered. "That area is taken care of by everyone who's not going to die." He closed his book and said, "I think I shall get drunk."

"Why?"

"Because I imagine that in a day or two I shall be very sick."

"What about your wife?"

"Died eighteen years ago. Good riddance. And there had better not be an afterlife." He rose very slowly from his chair and held his belly gently. He pushed softly in with his fingertips, and then he said, "I was afraid of that."

"What?" Mr. Flood responded quickly.

"My incision never really closed."

"What's that mean?"

"That your body can't heal itself properly, that you're starting to run down."

Within two days Mr. Miller developed a total body sickness ("the flu to the power of ten" he called it later) and his temperature went to 104.2° and stayed there for almost seventeen hours. Miss Scarli alerted the staff that Mr. Miller's death might be at hand, but when she came to check him he, if conscious, told her that under no circumstances would he die before he was good and goddamn ready. He was, even in the gross extremes of his illness, in control of his exacerbations, and he knew even before its onset that this particular one would not be his last.

But no one told Mr. Flood anything. The only exacerbation he had had was the relatively minor one that had brought him to his family doctor. He did not even know what the word meant, and the doctors and nurses were no help to him at all. During the first day Mr. Flood asked an intern what was wrong all of a sudden with Mr. Miller. The intern told him not to worry, he was in good hands. The evening nurse told Mr.

Going Gently

Flood that Mr. Miller's problem was that he had never taken care of himself in middle age. But it was Miss Scarli's statement that set Mr. Flood off. She said, "It's what happens, that's all." Shortly afterwards Mr. Flood began to show signs of every imaginable illness. His complaints to the doctors during morning rounds ranged from pounding headaches the night before to a tingling, warm sensation in the soles of his feet. Whatever medications were prescribed for Mr. Miller were requested by Mr. Flood. When they set up an I.V. for Mr. Miller, Mr. Flood asked if in fact he didn't need one, too. And after each injection for Mr. Miller, Mr. Flood was quick to call for one himself. When Mr. Miller's exacerbation was finally over, it was Mr. Flood who thought he had suffered more. Evidence of who had, though, was in Mr. Miller's face. There was a heavy, gray quality to it, as if the lines in it had been filled in with soot, and his eyes protruded like those of a giant insect. His lips were all but gone, his mouth shriveled into a dry slit.

Mr. Flood was watching him when he regained full consciousness. "You look pretty bad," Mr. Flood blurted.

"Thanks," came the almost inaudible response.

"Maybe you want some water or something, huh?" Mr. Flood said.

The sound Mr. Miller made was that of someone trying to spit tobacco off his tongue. But Mr. Flood saw his eyes widen and he brought him the water. Mr. Miller drank it very quickly and just as quickly vomited it all down his gown and bedsheet. Mr. Flood instantly rang for Miss Scarli, and when after a few minutes she did not come Mr. Flood tried to clean Mr. Miller's front. "Leave it," Mr. Miller said quietly, and Mr. Flood moved back to lean against his bed. Mr. Miller lay quietly in his own vomit; the only evidence of breathing was in the slight flapping sound of his cheeks and lips. Miss Scarli came to the room in twenty minutes. "My God, how long's it take you people, anyway?" Mr. Flood shouted at her.

"Two arms, two legs," she said. "You're hardly the only sick ones, you know."

Mr. Flood unfolded his arms and put his hands on the roll

Going Gently

of fat just above his hipbones. "But twenty minutes when a man's this sick," he said. "In an emergency."

"Throwing up is not an emergency," Mr. Miller said. He tried to pick his gown from his chest. "How long was it, Scarli?"

"Three days and a bit," she said to him.

"Not bad."

"But a strong one," she said. "Too damn strong for me."

"You'll get over it," he said. She pulled the sheet down from him and then reached behind his neck to untie the gown.

"God, you're a mess," she said when she removed the gown. His incision had oozed its fluid right through the bandages, and it sat in a yellowish half moon precisely in the middle of his belly.

"It's going to stink to high heaven," he said. Mr. Flood had turned away and was staring at the wall three feet from his face. Miss Scarli carefully changed Mr. Miller's dressing, and as she did so he said to her, "Why did it take you twenty minutes to get down here?"

"Coffee break," she said. "With cheese cake. One of the patients we discharged last week sent us some cheese cake."

"That's the reason I'm in love with you," Mr. Miller said. "You wouldn't move that granite behind of yours if Christ Himself were buzzing you."

"Not when there's cheese cake I wouldn't," she said.

"Nor I," Mr. Miller said.

She taped the corners of the heavy gauze to the edge of his bumpy ribs, and he asked her for some food. "Some juice and toast," she said, and she twirled the dirty gown inside the sheet and left the room.

"Is that what it's going to be like?" Mr. Flood said to the wall.

"For me," Mr. Miller said. "Everybody is different."

"You know what?" Mr. Flood said. "I feel great. That's the problem. It's like everyday I'm getting better."

"I'm not going to lie to you," Mr. Miller said.

"I know."

Going Gently

"You're going to fall like an oak tree."
"There's something about you, you know," Mr. Flood said.
"I'm a bastard."
"You certainly are."

Mr. Flood's first true exacerbation began a day and a half later. Its onset was furious. He was sitting in the chair by the foot of Mr. Miller's bed figuring in a checkbook he had asked his wife to bring. He suddenly set the checkbook down in his lap and looked wide-eyed at his bed across the room. His mouth fell open slightly and his forehead began to break into flowers of sweat. "Oh," he said in a private, soft way. He rose from the chair, the checkbook cartwheeling to the floor, and he started for his bed. He got to it just in time to vomit his breakfast right in the middle of it. He stared down at the soiled bed and began to whimper, "I got to lie down and I can't lie down." Then, "Oh," again in his way. Mr. Miller got out of bed slowly and painfully and shuffled toward Mr. Flood. Together they looked both sad and absurd. Mr. Miller, whose strength was concentrated wholly in his desire to stand up, was trying to turn Mr. Flood around and away from the bed. Sweat was pouring from Mr. Flood's face and he was not really aware of Mr. Miller. "I got to lie down," Mr. Flood said. Mr. Miller put his fingers into the inside of Mr. Flood's elbows and took his arms from the bed. He waddled him toward his own bed and Mr. Flood slumped across it. "You fat load," Mr. Miller hissed, and with his whole body shaking he rang for Miss Scarli. He stayed where he was, leaning against Mr. Flood so he would not slide from the bed, until Miss Scarli came in. "I don't care how long it takes you when I need you," Mr. Miller said to her, "but when you see his light from now on you had damn well better sprint."

Miss Scarli ignored Mr. Miller and went directly to help Mr. Flood. "What the hell's he doing on your bed?" she asked.

"He puked on his own,' Mr. Miller said. He half-staggered, half-pirouetted to the chair at the foot of his bed. Miss Scarli took the limp lower half of Mr. Flood's body and dropped it on the bed as if it were empty luggage. Then without looking at Mr. Miller she left the room hurriedly and returned with an orderly. Together they remade Mr. Flood's bed, and then they took him and half-carried, half-dragged him across the floor to it. "Damn it, be careful with him," Mr. Miller said.

"Back in bed, Homer," Miss Scarli said without looking up. Mr. Miller did so and as he pulled the sheet over himself he felt the warm place where Mr. Flood had been.

About an hour later, when they began to run I.V.'s into Mr. Flood to prevent what they said might be an electrolyte imbalance, Mr. Flood began to talk incoherently. At first Mr. Miller thought Mr. Flood was asking him questions, but as he concentrated on the sounds he realized that he was talking in his fever. "Glad, old pea," Mr. Flood said. "Bernie pea and Glady pea and a Gale pea and we all belong to the pea, pea pod." Then he gave a grotesque, husky chuckle as if he had globs of oil in his throat, and he made a series of repetitive sounds all of which were incomprehensible. "Shut up," Mr. Miller hurled from his bed.

"Huh?" Mr. Flood said, but he did not awaken. "Glady pea, Glady pea," he said.

"Shut up," Mr. Miller said again.

"Hot damn," he said very clearly, "bundle time again. Portsmouth . . . Kittery . . . Dover . . . Berwick. Portland by noon. If you get to Portland before noon, you didn't handle somebody right. Fuel at the diner by the viaduct. Eat good and line them up in a nice row for the afternoon. Fish in a barrel, Glady pea, they can't never resist me. It's the smile, don't you know, and it's holding their hand in the good firm shake for the extra second or two. Tells them you mean what you say. And I set them up, they don't even know it, like fish in a barrel, Glady pea, and I keep the loose-leaf binder under the seat in the car with all their talk from the last time, and I read it up just before the five deep breaths before I go in. Oh, but do I have them all lined up. They can't never resist me."

It was as if the clear, cold fluid entering his arm were some new kind of energy. He began to breathe with what in a

Going Gently

younger man would clearly have been sexual excitement. "I never missed but two or three in a whole virgin territory," he went on, "and I know it was my questions, my nine perfect questions. Nobody ever got past my questions. Like machine-gun fire and they were eating smack dab right out of my hand." His voice slipped and staggered in recollection of the questions, and for a few moments Mr. Miller heard only guttural sounds. But then Mr. Flood's body stiffened as though he were desperately trying to eject something intensely personal that had been locked inside him for years. "They were *mine*," he said, "*my* customers. I loved them, even the naturals, even the ones that got away." He paused and then said, "But I loved most of all the real sons of bitches."

Mr. Miller had long since rung for Miss Scarli, and when she came into the room he asked her to give Mr. Flood an injection. "Why?" she asked.

"Because he's out of his goddamn head," he said.

"What's he saying?" Miss Scarli asked.

"He's making me his priest, for Christ's sake."

Mr. Flood's exacerbation continued relentlessly. He fought the pain and the slamming sensations that went through him for just under a day. Then he gave up and let the thing run its course. In periods of semiconsciousness he called and called for water but no one gave him any. Occasionally Mr. Miller would tell him that he couldn't have any, but Mr. Flood did not hear him. The I.V.'s they ran did not stay even with Mr. Flood's loss of fluids, and he had periods when he felt he was shrinking. When he came out of the exacerbation after almost three days he had lost seventeen pounds. He gained back four of them within two days, but the other thirteen pounds were gone for good. When he was able to get up two days later he asked Mr. Miller if he had ever lost that kind of weight.

"No," Mr. Miller told him without looking up from his book.

"What's it mean?" Mr. Flood asked.

"Just gets you down to fighting weight," Mr. Miller said.

Going Gently

"How come I get it and you don't?"

"Don't you know anything about cancer?" Mr. Miller asked.

"If you got it, you know enough."

"Cute," Mr. Miller said. "Like a tough leading man."

"I guess you got everything there is to know about it somewhere in your head."

"As a matter of fact."

"What I'd like to know is why you know about it?" Mr. Flood said.

"Knowledge."

"What good is it?"

"It makes one understand," Mr. Miller said.

"Knowing things is all right," Mr. Flood said, "but when I know something and I can't use it I forget it. It don't mean a thing."

"Did you know cancer is as old as life itself?" Mr. Miller said. "When they told me I had the crab—that's where the disease originates its name from—I read very nearly twenty books within a week. The Greek in the original, the Egyptian and Sanskrit in translation of course. Fascinating. Fossil remnants of bones millions of years old reveal the honeycombing of carcinoma. Writings two thousand years before Christ make note of ulcers, mysterious swellings, tumors. "*Karkinos,*" he went on, loving the sound of his voice.

"What's that mean?" Mr. Flood asked from the edge of his bed.

"Crab," Mr. Miller said. "The Greek word for 'crab.' *Karkinos*, hence carcinoma. Crab because of the tentacle-like way the disease radiates throughout the body. Did you know that Galen, the great Roman physician, identified the cause of cancers as melancholia?"

"Can't say as I did."

"Rather putting the cart before the horse," Mr. Miller said, chuckling to himself.

"You really think that stuff's important?" Mr. Flood asked.

"It wasn't until the Renaissance that cancer got its first

serious scrutiny," Mr. Miller said. He raised the book slightly to indicate his source.

Mr. Flood looked hard across the room at Mr. Miller and then he said, "So what?"

Mr. Miller closed his book and after a moment said, "Good point."

The stench in the room the next morning was unmistakable. It was noticed first by Mr. Flood, who said across the room, "What in hell is that?" The orderly noticed it but said nothing when he brought the breakfast trays. But very soon Miss Scarli came in and went directly to Mr. Miller. "I have a day off and they don't even change your dressing," she said to him.

"Neglect is one of my minor difficulties," he answered and then lay back passively in the bed. Miss Scarli went to work quickly on him. His wound was noticeably larger, puckering up like a little volcano, and fluid ran freely from it for a few seconds after Miss Scarli took off the last layer of gauze. She cleaned the wound carefully, and when she asked Mr. Miller if he had pain he told her he did not. Mr. Flood drank his juice, but with the odor in the room as strong as it was, he quickly set the metal cover back over his plate of whitish scrambled eggs. As Miss Scarli finished her dressing on Mr. Miller, the orderly came in with an aerosol can of air freshener and set it down on Mr. Miller's night table. Then Miss Scarli stood right beside the bed and pulled the sheet to Mr. Miller's chin. She picked the can from the table and shook it vigorously. Then she blessed the air over Mr. Miller's bed and set the can down again and left the room.

Mr. Flood moved off his bed with a quick motion and went straight for the can. He took it and began to spray the entire room. White, misty clouds began to squirm out of the can and hang in the air. He sprayed and sprayed. "What are you doing?" Mr. Miller asked.

"Cleaning out the place," Mr. Flood answered. His arm completed a long arc.

Going Gently

"Will you please stop it?"

"I can still smell it."

"Then spray some up your nose," Mr. Miller said.

Mr. Flood spun around, the can still emptying itself, and said, "I don't stink."

"God has been good to you," Mr. Miller answered. He coughed as a billow of the heavily perfumed mist surrounded his chest and head. Mr. Flood stopped spraying then and tested the air with his nose. Then he noticed that the can was nearly empty, and he put the cap back on it and set it down on the night table. "Are you satisfied that the room has been purged of all offensive vapors?" Mr. Miller said.

"That's a God-awful smell you got there."

"I am closer to it than you are," Mr. Miller said quietly.

"Why'd it all of a sudden get like that?"

"Because they did not change the dressing," Mr. Miller answered.

"If that was me, I'd sure as hell let them know a thing or two."

"It would do no good."

Mr. Flood thought for a moment and then said, "Why don't people come in here more? I see so many people going up and down the hall."

"It allows us more time for self-pity," Mr. Miller said.

"Nobody every really comes in here," Mr. Flood said, as if discovering a truth.

Both men slept well for most of the afternoon, and when Mr. Miller awakened along toward five he sat up in his bed and stared in horror at a twenty-seven inch color television set that sat between the beds. There was a bright red ribbon around it with an envelope attached at the bow. "Flood!" he shouted. "Wake up and tell me who in the name of God has given birth to *that*."

Mr. Flood slowly came alive, and he looked with wonder at the television. "Jesus, damn," he said, and he smiled affectionately at the set.

Going Gently

"Well," Mr. Miller said.

"Beats me," Mr. Flood answered.

"Get the goddamn thing out of here," Mr. Miller said. He pointed to it as if it were a deadly animal.

Mr. Flood eased himself out of bed and went to the set. He rubbed his hand over the top of it, and then he fondled the knobs as if he were a child with a Christmas toy. "Jesus, that's nice," he said to himself.

"Flood, what the hell are you doing?" Mr. Miller said. "Out of this room with that."

Mr. Flood took no notice. He pulled the envelope from the ribbon, and when he saw his name on it he turned it over and opened it. A card inside read, "With all my love, Daddy. Gale." And underneath it his son had carefully printed:

DO NOT GO GENTLE INTO THAT
GOOD NIGHT.
RAGE, RAGE AGAINST THE DYING OF
THE LIGHT.

Mr. Flood read the card several times, and his bewilderment was visible on his face.

"Well," Mr. Miller said again.

"Shut up," Mr. Flood said quietly, and he put the card to his chest with great affection.

"Who in hell has perpetrated this on me?" Mr. Miller said.

"It's from my son, from his shop, the card says."

"His shop?" Mr. Miller said.

"Gale's Gale."

"Whatever is a Gale's Gale?"

"His boutique, or whatever you call it," Mr. Flood said. He looked down again at the card like a poker player.

"Dandy," Mr. Miller said. "Now, when is this monstrosity going to leave?"

"You are a sad son of a bitch," Mr. Flood said vehemently. "It's just because you ain't got nobody that you don't want me to have my family. Well, Mr. Professor Big

Going Gently

Shot, it stays. And if you don't like it, you can lump it."

"I shall kick its face in." Mr. Miller said.

"You do and I shall kick in yours right after it."

Mr. Miller's little body was afire. Reason had suddenly deserted him and he was helpless without it. He yanked his buzzer from the night table and started squeezing it as if he might make some final statement with it. When Miss Scarli came into the room Mr. Miller was still holding the buzzer, and Mr. Flood was unwrapping the ribbon around the television. "What have we here?" she said to Mr. Flood.

"Scarli, you're a reasonable woman," Mr. Miller said.

"Sometimes," she said, and then she looked back to the television. "Your son didn't want to wake you," she said to Mr. Flood.

"He was here? He brought it himself?"

"He came with the two men who brought it," she said.

"Reason, Scarli, I beg of you," Mr. Miller put in.

She turned slowly toward Mr. Miller as she said, "What's the trouble, Homer?"

"You know perfectly well."

"I can understand your objections to the last black and white," she said. "But this is color." She spread her arms in emphasis.

"What little respect I had for you as a human being has abated," he said.

"You want the rule sheets brought out again?"

"I know what the rules say," Mr. Miller answered. "They say he can have his sleek full-color fruit carton if he pleases to. And, furthermore, they say that if the other patient in the room doesn't care for fruit cartons, it is simply his eternal bad luck."

"You two can work it out," she said, and as she started to leave the room she looked again at the set.

"It's all right, isn't it?" Mr. Flood said.

"Play it day and night if you want," she answered.

"I'll get you for that, Scarli," Mr. Miller said.

Going Gently

"When are you going to join the twentieth century?" she said to him.

"Never."

There was a long moment of silence in the room after Miss Scarli left. Mr. Miller toyed with his buzzer and Mr. Flood began to unwrap the cord from the back of the television. He held it in his hands for a few seconds while his eyes moved about the walls of the room in search of a socket. His gaze settled on the outlet just above Mr. Miller's head and he started for it. "You wouldn't dare," Mr. Miller said to him.

"No?"

"Take one more step and I'll let you have it," Mr. Miller said. He slapped the buzzer into his palm as though it were a blackjack. "There's an outlet just behind the head of your bed," he said. "You had better use that." Then he very deliberately pressed the buzzer and reached into the cabinet of the night table and took out the whisky bottle.

"Going to get drunk?" Mr. Flood asked.

"Utterly."

Mr. Flood began to pull the rabbit ears up from the back of the set, and as he did so he said, "What you got against T.V., anyway? T.V. helps to pass the time."

"That's the first thing I've got against it," Mr. Miller answered. The orderly brought in a fresh pitcher of ice water and set it on Mr. Miller's night table. As he was leaving the room he paused for just an instant to watch the television blossom into a painfully green existence. Then he was gone and Mr. Flood turned to Mr. Miller and said, "How do you get the green out?" He stooped a little to look at the array of knobs on the right side of the set.

"Green people are rather refreshing" Mr. Miller said. He poured the ice water into the whisky and drank two large gulps. Mr. Flood began to turn the knobs in a random, awkward way, and the picture whirled down the color spectrum and back with great speed. "Is there a dial that says 'Tint'?" Mr. Miller asked.

"Here it is," Mr. Flood said after a moment. He began to

55

Going Gently

turn it as if he were rapidly winding a watch, and the picture went so green that only the vague outlines of the faces were distinguishable.

"The other way, boob," Mr. Miller said.

"Who you calling . . . " Mr. Flood began, but then the picture began to adjust itself under the ramblings of his fingers, and he forgot what he was going to say.

"Is it possible that we might watch a news broadcast?" Mr. Miller asked.

"I want to see what else is on," Mr. Flood said. He twirled the channel selector so fast that all of the stations seemed to blur into one. Mr. Miller rolled his eyes to the ceiling and then took another large mouthful of whisky.

The television sat between the beds all that evening as if it were a short, square person for whom Mr. Flood had great affection. Mr. Miller tried to read but it was impossible. He drank in an effort to block the meaningless gurgles and burps that spilled from the set onto the floor of the room. When he could stand it no longer he asked Mr. Flood to turn the set down to minimum volume. Mr. Flood turned the set only a little bit lower and moved forward. Then after a while Mr. Miller would ask again and Mr. Flood would comply. By ten-thirty that evening Mr. Flood was no more than two feet from the set, and Mr. Miller was good and filled up with whisky. But he knew it, and he was not surprised to hear his own voice slur occasionally, or to feel his hand slip a little on the side of the glass when he went to pick it from the night table. He knew that he was very close to being very drunk, but he did not care about it. There was the feeling in him of deep depression, as if the organs of his body had suddenly gone to rocks, and he felt an isolation from his surroundings, a distance from Mr. Flood and the rest of his small world. He picked his glass from the table and sat it on his chest, within tipping distance of his lips, and he stared alternately at Mr. Flood and his television set. He watched Mr. Flood giggle occasionally at the program he was watching, and when he did Mr. Miller's head went slowly back and forth in awe and

Going Gently

bewilderment. Finally, without thinking about it, he said, "When are you going to turn that thing off?" Mr. Flood answered him with a short wave of his hand, as if he were batting away a fly. *"When?"* Mr. Miller said. He waited for an answer but none came. Mr. Flood simply reached out and adjusted the volume upwards. Again Mr. Miller asked him, and this time Mr. Flood said, "You drink too much." He giggled at the program and said, "Did you see, that? Jesus damn, that was funny."

"It was not funny," Mr. Miller said. A comic magician had appeared to swallow two Ping-Pong balls.

"It was to me," Mr. Flood said. He did not move his eyes from the set.

"How in the name of God can you look at that thing for hours upon end?"

"I like it," Mr. Flood said.

"Can't you read a book or talk or something?"

"I never liked reading," Mr. Flood said to the set.

Mr. Miller drank himself into a half sleep within the next hour, and Mr. Flood moved back in his bed to watch the late movies. He was soon sound asleep and the television continued to throw its rainbow in eerie fashion about the walls of the room. All the while, Mr. Miller kept his glass balanced on his chest, and he watched the television through half-opened eyelids. When he heard Mr. Flood begin to snore in what sounded a most profound and satisfied way, he got out of bed and went to the television. He was about to turn it off when he saw the card laying on the top of the set. He picked it up and read what Mr. Flood's son had written:

> DO NOT GO GENTLE INTO THAT
> GOOD NIGHT,
> RAGE, RAGE AGAINST THE DYING OF
> THE LIGHT.

The hand that held the card dropped to his side and he turned to look at Mr. Flood's sleeping form. "Oh, no, Flood,"

Going Gently

he said very softly, "this hasn't got it at all." He shook his head slowly and said, "It isn't even close." He put the card back on top of the television and turned it off.

The next morning when Mr. Flood put the television on at a quarter past six the picture filled only half the screen. In ten minutes it had shrunk to the size of a postcard, and in another ten minutes there was a dry, crackling sound and the picture tube blew.

THREE

It was after breakfast that the painters arrived—two short, tired men not much younger than Mr. Miller and Mr. Flood. They came into the room with an air of familiarity, much like anybody else who worked at the hospital, and Mr. Miller and Mr. Flood watched in amazement as the men ignored them and went about putting their drop cloths and small ladders in place. When Mr. Miller finally realized that he was not going to receive even the barest of greetings from the men, much less an explanation as to why they had suddenly occupied the room, he addressed them quietly: "What do you think you two are doing?" The shorter of the two painters glanced up at Mr. Miller, then at his partner, and shook his head in a private communication. "You there," Mr. Miller said, and his arm flashed out and pointed at the man, "explain yourself." The painter turned and looked at the number on the door. Then he said to Mr. Miller, "We're supposed to be here today."

"On whose authorization?"

Going Gently

"It's on the schedule," the man said, and he began to stir the paint slowly.

"Whose bloody schedule?"

"Don't know," the man said. "Every year come this time in November we do the five rooms along this side." His hand made a sweeping gesture with the five-inch brush.

"And what do you do, say, in the last week in April?"

"All April's the operating rooms," the man said. "We got to work nights then."

His partner nodded and said, "No differential, neither."

"And what may I ask do you do if you go into a room, *barge* into a room I might add, and discover someone critically ill?"

"Work around him," the painter said.

It was then that the orderly and Miss Scarli came to the door of the room, and behind them Mr. Miller and Mr. Flood saw the two wheelchairs. With her thumb in the air like a determined hitchhiker, Miss Scarli gave the order for the two men to leave the room. Mr. Miller and Mr. Flood put on their robes slowly and shuffled to the wheelchairs. Just before they were wheeled away, Mr. Miller said to the painters, "When do you anticipate finishing?"

"Standard-sized room," the painter said. "They all take three hours and ten minutes."

"Move this cart, Scarli," Mr. Miller said. "Before I lose control of myself."

The two men were wheeled to the day lounge at the end of the hall on the far side of the nurses' station. When they were left alone Mr. Flood looked about the room and said, "Do you play cards?"

"Course I play cards," Mr. Miller said. His eyes darted from corner to corner as if looking for an object on which to release his anger.

"Poker?" Mr. Flood said, and with effort he wheeled himself to a cardtable.

"Anything you like," Mr. Miller said, and then, after

Going Gently

another moment of looking about, he backed his wheelchair to the table and adeptly spun around.

"You realize, of course, that you need brains to play poker."

"Dry up," Mr. Flood said. "Three-card draw?"

"Whatever."

"How you been feeling?" Mr. Flood asked as he shuffled the cards and then offered the cut to Mr. Miller.

"Rotten," Mr. Miller said. He slapped the top half of the deck on the table and then completed the cut.

"I weighed myself yesterday," Mr. Flood said as he dealt.

"And?"

"Down eight more pounds."

"Feeling weaker?"

"Some. Not too much." The cards floated soundlessly down from his hands and slid like secrets one upon another. "You?"

"I should imagine that I'm due for my first thoracentesis," Mr. Miller said.

"How many?"

"Two, please."

"What's that?" Mr. Flood asked.

"They take a needle and stick it in your side—an enormous needle, I should underscore—and they drain fluid from your lungs."

"Dealer takes one." Mr. Flood snapped a card from the top of the deck. "It ain't good when it gets to your lungs."

"What have you got?"

"I filled the straight," Mr. Flood said proudly. He spread his cards like a fan in front of him.

"Chances for that are one in twelve," Mr. Miller said.

"Did you fill your flush?"

"Certainly," Mr. Miller said, putting his cards on top of Mr. Flood's.

"How long you got when it gets to your lungs?" Mr. Flood asked as he raked the cards together.

"Who the hell knows?" Mr. Miller said.

"Three-card draw again?" Mr. Flood asked. He slid the deck to Mr. Miller.

Going Gently

"It'll be a long time before you fill another straight," Mr. Miller said. He dealt slowly and mechanically. He gently tossed a card at Mr. Flood, and then he peeked at the corner of the one he gave himself. When he was done he left his cards on the table and looked at Mr. Flood, who was in deep concentration on his hand.

"How do you know when it gets to your lungs?" Mr. Flood said without looking up.

"Continual, severe pressure around the diaphragm," Mr. Miller said. "This morning there were a few spots of blood on the pillow, salty taste in the mouth. All very textbook."

"Three, please," Mr. Flood said.

"Dealer stands," Mr. Miller said. Mr. Flood looked up quickly and told Mr. Miller he was bluffing.

"I am," Mr. Miller said.

"All right then, I call," Mr. Flood said. "A pair of eights." He put the cards down.

"You win," Mr. Miller said. He put his cards into the pile without showing them to Mr. Flood.

"What'd you have?"

"Fives," he said.

"My deal," Mr. Flood said. Slowly he began to shuffle the cards, but his motions quickly became very deliberate and direct, and it was clear that his ability to concentrate was lessening.

"Diarrhea?" Mr. Miller asked.

"Mr. Flood nodded slightly, his eyes riveted to the cards. "How'd you know?"

"I live in the same room," Mr. Miller said.

"Sometimes it burns like crazy."

"How many times a day?"

"Six, eight."

"Have you told anybody?"

"Everybody," Mr. Flood said. His face was gray. "And all they do is write it down on the goddamn charts."

"Will you be all right?"

"It'll pass," he said, and then Mr. Miller watched Mr. Flood

Going Gently

finally gain control of himself. His face relaxed and he said, "Stud?" He dealt three rounds, and when he saw that Mr. Miller had three fours he folded from the hand.

"I haven't seen your wife for six days now," Mr. Miller said as he gathered in the cards.

"She went to tell my mother about me," Mr. Flood said.

"Anything to get away," Mr. Miller answered. "Is she well?"

"Better than most at eighty-nine," Mr. Flood said. "She says she can do anything but travel."

"Living to eighty-nine," Mr. Miller said. "Another twenty-two years."

"I'd give anything for that," Mr. Flood said.

"Not me," Mr. Miller said flatly.

"Why's that?"

"I shall retract that remark by noon," Mr. Miller said.

"Jesus, don't you ever get scared?"

"I am in a state of continual, abject panic," Mr. Miller said.

"But you never show it."

"Good mask," Mr. Miller said. He shuffled.

"Jesus, you're cocky," Mr. Flood said. "You sit there cool as a cucumber with everything locked up inside you." He looked hard at Mr. Miller. "Is there anybody who knows how you really feel?"

"The only person I can think of is you."

"Deal."

They did not agree to stop playing cards. It was as though the game were a third person at the table who quietly slipped away during conversation. After Mr. Flood had another mild attack of diarrhea they wheeled themselves toward a large bay window across the room. The view from the window was away from the town and shoreline and toward the gradual gray rise of worn mountains in the distance. They sat for a few moments looking at the window as if it were a movie screen on which nothing would ever play. In the near distance there were a few houses on squared-off blocks, a gas station, two billboards with the same political ad. Then in the far distance

Going Gently

they saw where the gently rising land came together with fat gray clouds in a vague and uncertain line. They did not speak for a long time. Mr. Flood's gaze was blank and useless, but Mr. Miller's eyes ran hard and fast along the window as if he were trying to see something that was not there. Finally he said with a measure of triumph in his voice, "There, there it is, I thought so."

"What?"

"Snow," Mr. Miller said.

"Where?" Mr. Flood asked as if he had never seen any.

"Two flakes," Mr. Miller said. His hand was raised, two fingers crookedly extended, and he traced in the air the path the flakes had made.

"I don't see any."

"Yes, they were there," Mr. Miller said more in excitement than in an effort to convince.

"I didn't see them, I tell you." Mr. Flood turned toward Mr. Miller, and as he did Mr. Miller's hand shot out again and Mr. Flood turned back to the window just in time to see two more flakes settling down in unison against the large pane. He watched them flutter down against the outside metal sill and then dissolve abruptly into two small drops. Quickly he looked back up the length of the pane for more snow, but his eyes swept its surface in vain. "Well, Jesus, what's it going to do?" he said to Mr. Miller.

"Give it time," Mr. Miller said.

After a few minutes the snow began, and when the men tired of looking closely at the individual flakes as they swirled against the window, they looked again into the far distance, where the snow had already begun to cover up the blank hills.

"It's not going to last," Mr. Miller said after a few minutes.

"The hell you say," Mr. Flood shot at him.

"Don't get your hopes up."

"Look how hard it's coming down," Mr. Flood said.

"That's the problem," Mr. Miller said.

"What do you think for accumulation?" They turned to face each other.

Going Gently

"Nothing but a trace."

"Hell, man, it'll be a foot anyhow," Mr. Flood said.

"Not in the first week in November it won't," Mr. Miller said. "And the wind isn't right, to boot."

"It's not so much what you say, you know," Mr. Flood said. "It's your goddamn attitude."

Then together they looked back to the window and saw that the snow had stopped as suddenly as it had come, and there was only a soft layer along the outside sill to indicate that it had snowed at all.

"A study of weather, albeit on a most amateurish basis, has consumed my spare time for a number of years," Mr. Miller said. He stretched a little way out of the chair as though to observe more closely the conditions outside. "In fact, had I my life to live over, I think I would have been a competent meteorologist."

"You can have it," Mr. Flood said. "Goddamn northeasters never did nothing for me except make me late somewhere."

"And would you be a salesman if you could do it all again?" Mr. Miller asked.

"No," Mr. Flood said, and there was an unfamiliar gentleness in his voice. "I think maybe I'd be me a vet, a veterinarian." There was a lazy, summer quality to his voice.

"Curious."

"I loved animals all my life," Mr. Flood went on. "All kinds, never did matter." He paused in his remembrance and then said, "Even when I was first traveling and there weren't all the hot-shot superhighways I used to stop a lot by the farms and whatnot just to watch the animals. And zoos," he said and laughed to himself, "ain't a zoo in any town where I been that I haven't seen. Maybe I'd be me a zoo keeper or something like that."

"The money's no good," Mr. Miller said.

"The money stinks," Mr. Flood said. He smiled in a way that made his face truly warm and appealing.

"So we would both deal with natural phenomena had we the opportunity to do it all again."

Going Gently

"When you're around animals you know your place," Mr. Flood said.

"Man has been most misguided in his superior attitude over the animal world," Mr. Miller said.

"Could you just for once hold back on the bilge?" Mr. Flood said. "Honest to God, I think that maybe if I said the sky is falling, you'd have to tell me about cloud formations."

"I probably would," Mr. Miller said. "Or at least I'd have a shot at it."

The men sat for some time and they neither spoke nor moved. They looked as if they would sit there until their bodies froze into statues. Finally Miss Scarli and the orderly interrupted their privacy, and for Mr. Flood it was none too soon. They got him back to his room just as a violent attack of diarrhea struck, and when Miss Scarli became aware that it was diarrhea she promptly left the room. "Earn your money," Mr. Miller said to the orderly as he closed the curtains and went to work on Mr. Flood. After a few moments of silence Mr. Miller heard Mr. Flood say to the orderly, "Is it still snowing out?"

"I didn't know it was snowing at all," he answered. "The radio didn't say anything about it snowing."

"Well, it did," Mr. Flood said.

"Turn over."

Mr. Miller lay quietly in his bed and listened to the sounds that came from Mr. Flood's side of the room. Then he began to cough softly, a low, easy convulsing that rolled liquid into his bronchial tubes, where it stayed for a moment gurgling. Then he coughed harder, the fluid bubbling toward the back of his throat, and he gagged slightly. He reached out and took the kidney shaped metal pan and put it to the side of his mouth. In one hard spasm of his upper body he expelled stringy, yellowish-red fluid into the pan. Then he truly began to cough, and when Mr. Flood asked if he was all right he said, "Yes, damn it."

"You okay?" the orderly asked.

"Yes, damn it," Mr. Miller said. he turned and pressed his face into the pillow to muffle the next spasm.

The orderly stopped his work on Mr. Flood just long enough to reach out and pres the call button. When Miss Scarli came into the room the orderly stepped out from behind Mr. Flood's curtain and quietly said to her, "He's coughing his head off. Can't stop." She went quickly to Mr. Miller and as she did he lifted his face from the stained pillow to look at her. "No good, Scarli," he said and rolled a little onto his side. She took the pan and the pillow and set them on the chair at the end of the bed. "I didn't mind it so much when I didn't know where it was," he said. "Then it was all theory, all abstract." He tried to smile.

"What can I do?" she asked.

"Stop the coughing," he said. "Please."

"I can do it, but only for a while," she said.

"Do it," he said, and she saw him relax. "And for God's sake, give Flood something for his gut."

Within half an hour both men were heavily medicated and asleep, but even as he slept Mr. Miller's body jerked now and again very slightly.

In a few hours the men were awake and both were nauseated slightly by the smell of fresh paint in the room. Mr. Miller lay on his back with his breathing under control, and Mr. Flood huddled down in his bed with the sheet pressed to his face. Both men looked very tired. "The fumes are murder," Mr. Flood said. Mr. Miller raised a hand from the bed to indicate that he had heard, and after a few moments he very slowly pulled himself into a sitting position. He rubbed his hand across his chest in a deliberate way, as though to examine himself, and then he forced a cough. He felt the fluids in the lower part of his chest rumble a little, but they seemed somehow inactive for the present, somehow like resting lava. He took the can of aerosol spray and aimed it in Mr. Flood's direction. "You're a big help," Mr. Flood said. He wiped his forehead with the sheet.

Going Gently

"Because of you I didn't get any lunch," Mr. Miller said.

"The way you were coughing you couldn't have eaten anyway," Mr. Flood said.

"And we've slept through the orderly's rounds," Mr. Miller said.

"Frankly, I can do without it," Mr. Flood said. "Food and me, we ain't getting on so well."

"It won't be long to dinner."

But dinner came and went and the men heard only the sounds of trays being rattled on and off the carts in the hall. They waited patiently, each upright on the edge of his bed, each with his table pulled in front of him. They heard the orderlies and the nurses' aides come and go from the other rooms, and it was not until full silence fell on the hall that Mr. Miller cursed and pressed his call button. Finally, after almost half an hour, a young nurse whom neither man had ever seen put her head into the room and asked if there was something they wanted. "My goddamn dinner," Mr. Miller said slowly and with great authority.

"What kind of shop you running, lady?" Mr. Flood said, and he looked at Mr. Miller. The nurse told them that she had no idea what they were talking about but that she would tell Mrs. Marvin. She came into the room fifteen minutes later, and as she whirled through the door she said, "Which one of you swore at a member of my staff?"

"Listen, you withered old bitch," Mr. Miller said. "I have had enough of you. I really have. Mr. Flood and I did not receive dinner this evening."

"What do you think that has to do with me?" she asked. Her eyes narrowed down and her small body became erect for full combat.

"Damn it, woman, you're in charge, aren't you?" Mr. Miller said.

"My jurisdiction hardly includes the dietitians," she said.

"There is, then, no explanation?"

"Did you fill out your menus this morning?" she asked.

"They were painting our room," Mr. Flood put in.

Going Gently

"No menu, no dinner," Mrs. Marvin said flatly.
"Now, what the hell?" Mr. Flood said.
"If no menu is filled out, no dinner is prepared," she said complacently.
"You would have made a perfect Nazi," Mr. Miller said.
"What are you going to do?" Mr. Flood asked, his voice riding over Mr. Miller's remark.
"Perhaps when the orderly makes his evening rounds," she said, and her eyes did not move from Mr. Miller, "perhaps then you may have some toast."
"Cinnamon," Mr. Miller said, "and lightly buttered."
"By all means."

They sat on the edges of the beds for a few moments after Mrs. Marvin left the room, and then Mr. Miller looked up at Mr. Flood and said, "Jesus, how I love a fight." He brought his arm around as if he were conducting a symphony.
"I think I see why your wife died so young," Mr. Flood said, and for the first time since his operation Mr. Miller laughed long and hard. When he was finished there were tears in his eyes. Then Mr. Flood said quietly, "How do you feel? I mean from this afternoon."
"Afternoons are always the worst," he said.
Mr. Flood nodded his understanding and said, "I was thinking we might have some whisky."
"You're all right, Mr. Flood," Mr. Miller said, and he pushed the table away and slid off the bed. He got the whisky bottle and poured some into Mr. Flood's glass and then half-filled his own. They drank and then there was a long moment while each waited to see what the effect of the whisky would be. Mr. Flood's face flushed and he shut his eyes tight. Mr. Miller's mouth opened as if for a kiss and he closed his eyes in sheer delight.
But then the normal effects of the whisky telescoped and the men quickly felt first and second uplifts. Mr. Miller drank the rest of his glass and refilled it. Mr. Flood was slower and

more cautious. "I'm going to get that goddamn bitch," Mr. Miller said.

"Do you think this'll mess up my gut?" Mr. Flood asked as he raised his glass.

"No, it's a depressant," Mr. Miller said. "It slows up everything."

Mr. Flood put the glass to his mouth in a firm motion. "I haven't been drunk in a long, long time," he said.

"Clean liver," Mr. Miller said.

"My only bad habits was cigars and coffee," Mr. Flood said. "You think coffee can give you cancer?"

"Certainly," Mr. Miller said. He drank again.

"Jesus, I could use me something to eat," Mr. Flood said.

"Drink," Mr. Miller answered. He handed the bottle to Mr. Flood.

"You sure this stuff is okay for my gut?"

"Cement couldn't hurt it."

Mr. Flood half-filled his glass and sipped from it, and his body shuddered slightly at the biter taste. His frame bent and sagged noticeably, as if his back bone had suddenly weakened, and he stared into the glass. "It stinks," he said after a moment. "It's a goddamn son-of-a-bitching rotten deal."

"Get off it," Mr. Miller said.

"The hell with you, I got a right."

"Agreed," Mr. Miller said. "But you keep it to yourself."

"There you go again."

"If I had had, say, a hemorrhoid operation," Mr. Miller said, "and I was forced to lie on an inflated little life preserver while you bemoaned your fate, I would have a moral obligation to listen to your self-pity. However, as it stands, we have no responsibility to the other. Weak grammar there." He looked at his glass.

"All I said was it's a rotten deal."

"But we know that," Mr. Miller answered. "Debating the degree is idiocy."

"Well, Jesus," Mr. Flood said vehemently, "what's a guy supposed to do?"

"Depends on the guy," Mr. Miller said, and he drank from his glass.

"You really think you're tough, don't you?"

Mr. Miller smiled to himself and said, "If I let you talk my-head off about how you feel, you're obligated to do the same for me. It makes little sense for two grown men to dribble off at the mouth about how life has suddenly cheated the be-Jesus out of them."

"I suppose you'd like to talk about the history of cancer," Mr. Flood said.

"No," Mr. Miller answered quietly. He sipped again and finally said, "If you want to know the truth, I was thinking about what I'm going to miss."

"What you're going to *miss?*" Mr. Flood chuckled. "You can't miss nothing when you're dead."

"Can't you?"

"Hell, no."

"May I tell you what I'm going to miss?"

"Be my guest," Mr. Flood said, and he made a sweeping gesture with his arm.

"Shakespeare, Twain, Beethoven's Seventh, Titian," he said very rapidly. Then after a brief moment, "Browning, Cubism, biographies." He stopped and looked at Mr. Flood. "All of them," he said, "but most of all irony and paradox."

"You teachers," Mr. Flood said.

"It's ideas, you see," Mr. Miller said, his hands holding two invisible melons. "Ideas."

"What's such a big deal about ideas?" Mr. Flood said. "An idea is symmetrical," Mr. Miller said, "and that symmetry is exactly the thing I shall miss."

"I don't know one word of what you're saying," Mr. Flood said. "It's where things fit, where they go together and work harmoniously." He thought for a moment and then said, "It's where you suddenly see that things belong to each other. Where they mesh like hands in prayer."

"If you say so," Mr. Flood said.

"I'm sorry."

Going Gently

"It's all right, it sounds great," Mr. Flood said.
"Here," Mr. Miller said. He poured more whisky into Mr. Flood's glass. Mr. Flood looked down at it and mumbled to himself that he shouldn't be drinking so much, and Mr. Miller told him he was absolutely right.

When the orderly brought the juices the young nurse followed him into the room with several pieces of toast on a small paper plate. She set them down on Mr. Miller's table, and as she was about to leave Mr. Miller said to her, "How long have you been exposed to the cruel and inhuman tutelage of Mrs. Marvin?" Mr. Flood was shaking his head. The nurse kept her eyes on the plate as she said, "Tomorrow will be two weeks." Mr. Miller saw clearly that the girl was uncomfortable. "Let me introduce myself," he said. "I am Professor Miller and that is Mr. Flood."

She nodded her head slowly and after a minute she said, "I know."

"Is that why you've been avoiding this room?" he asked her.

The directness of the question seemed to go right through her and she blurted, "We flip . . . it's not that I didn't want to come in. It's just . . . " and her voice trailed off like a billow of dust.

"You what?" Mr. Flood said. The girl kept her head down and she stood as if she had no clothes on.

"They flip coins," Mr. Miller said to him quietly. "To see who has to take care of us."

"Goddamn," Mr. Flood said more in surprise than anger.

"Whatever do they teach you in your schools?" Mr. Miller asked her, but he let the question go when he saw that the girl's composure was crumbling fast.

Mr. Flood was not so generous. "Who the hell do you think you are?" he said. "I'm no Christmas turkey in your damn raffle. You're getting damn good money to take care of us," he fumbled on, his anger inexpressible. "Jesus damn," he said and his lips set in a tight red line.

"It's just that I don't know what to do," the girl blurted.

Going Gently

She looked up at Mr. Miller and then she pushed her hands deep into her uniform pockets and said, "I don't know how to take care of you."

"My dear," Mr. Miller said as gently as he possibly could, "all any of us really wants to do is talk."

"Nobody on the whole floor wants to come in here," she said. Her head was still down, her eyes closed.

"Just take the time to listen to us," he said.

"Everybody knows it's the worst duty in the place," she said.

"And suppose we had leprosy?" Mr. Flood threw in.

"I could take care of that," the girl said. She turned toward Mr. Flood. "I could really take care of that."

"Get out," Mr. Flood said. "Go on, out."

"I'm so sorry," she said. She went quickly for the door.

"I hope she gets hers some day," Mr. Flood said after she had left the room.

"Be kind, Flood," Mr. Miller said. "The girl is troubled."

"My heart bleeds."

The next morning the men were very sick. Their exacerbations had begun in the night and the severity of them went unnoticed until the night nurse took the early-morning temperatures. Mr. Flood's was 104.6° and Mr. Miller's a flat 105°. When Miss Scarli saw that recorded on Mr. Miller's chart she came directly to the room. She immediately checked both men's vital signs and then retook the temperatures. They were holding at the same levels. As she made her notes Mr. Miller barely regained consciousness. When he saw her he said, "This one is a bitch."

"How do you feel?" she asked.

"Like someone set me on fire," he said.

"I bet you do," she said, looking at the thermometer.

"A hundred five degrees."

'You shouldn't tell me that," he said.

"That's for me to decide."

"How's Flood?" he asked.

"About the same as you."

Going Gently

"Is this the last one?" Mr. Miller said. In his voice there was a hint of true panic.

"Maybe," she said. "I don't know. Not for Mr. Flood anyhow."

"Good for you, Scarli," Mr. Miller said.

"You know I'm not going to lie to you," she said.

"Did it take you long to learn that?" he asked, and when she smiled down at him he suddenly said, "Have someone sit with us today. Anyone, it doesn't matter." His voice was light and fast. "I know you're short," he said. "You're always short. Anyone will do. A blind deaf-mute will do."

"I'll try,' she said. "But no promises."

"Get the I.V.'s going," Mr. Miller said. "Flood's weight loss last time was atrocious."

Mr. Miller stayed conscious until Miss Scarli returned and began the necessary procedures. He watched her and the orderly work on Mr. Flood and then come back to his bed to administer medication and set up the I.V. next to the night table. When he told Miss Scarli not to stick him with the IV needle until he was out again, she told him he could go to hell. He turned his left arm over and offered it to her like candy. When she could not get the needle into the vein after repeated efforts she told the orderly to make up a cut-down set and tell one of the nurses to put in a call for a resident. "Is it me or you?" Mr. Miller asked her. She told him she didn't know. She took the blood pressure cuff from the tray, and when she finally got a reading on him she said, "It's both of us. There should be just enough pressure in that thing." She ran her finger along the inside of his arm. "But I'm damned if I can get into it."

"I don't want them to cut down to it," Mr. Miller said. "Stick it yourself. Spear and jab until you get it. Come on, now, you do it."

She took a fresh needle and went to the inside of his elbow. She slipped the tip of it under his skin and then looked up to his face. He was watching her progress intently, his face absolutely motionless. He continued to watch as Miss Scarli felt

Going Gently

for the vein with the point of the needle. "Homer," she said after several tries, "it's rolling on me. I can get the tip right on it and then it rolls."

"You do it," he said.

Miss Scarli tried one more time, and when she had the vein pinned down with the end of the needle she pushed forward slightly and the needle went right through the vein. The lump of the hematoma began to rise almost immediately, and neither of them moved as they watched the punctured vein bleed under the skin.

"Nice going," he said to her. She removed the needle from his arm and then grabbed his elbow as if it were a baseball. As she applied hard pressure to the swelling Mr. Miller said to her, "Now they'll have to cut down to it."

"It's not going to hurt a lot," she said.

"It's that I have to look at it," he said. "It's evidence." His head rolled away from her.

"Homer," she said in a flat, dull voice with no meaning.

"Give me theory," he said half to the wall. "Abstractions, the whole unseen world. Give me that. But don't cut into my arm because my veins are shutting down." He paused for a moment and closed his eyes. "I can see that." Then the medication began to take effect and Mr. Miller drifted into a hard sleep.

He awakened several times during the afternoon, and each time he did he looked first at his arm and then to Mr. Flood. Then he checked to see if there was a sitter in the room. The first time he saw the orderly reading a comic book, the second time Miss Scarli herself, and along toward late afternoon he saw that the sitter was the young nurse from the previous evening. "Lose the toss again?" he asked through dry, waxy lips.

"They said you'd stay asleep," she said.

"I'm sure they did."

"I volunteered," she said, answering his question.

"Suppose you and me, we get a six-pack," he said.

Going Gently

"I've heard about your drinking," she said. She rose and came toward him.

"You're very pretty," he said. "How old are you?" She told him she was twenty. "I suppose you're tired of people telling you you've got your whole life ahead of you?" he said. She nodded and smiled down at him. "Well," he said, and for a moment his mouth hung open like a derelict's and his eyes left hers and wandered about the ceiling. Finally he said, "I forgot. I forgot what I was going to say." He looked back to her and said with all the energy left in his small body, "Does that mean it's finally getting my brain?"

"I don't know," the girl said.

"There's two things I don't want, you see," he said, and he looked at her hard. "I don't mind the dying business, understand that, young lady. It's how. I don't want to die alone, that's one. And I don't want it to make boiled rice out of my brain. That's all." He lay back then, exhausted, and after a moment he looked up to the girl and said, "You get the feeling after a while that you'd like to make a deal with someone—anyone. Doesn't matter."

All the while Mr. Miller was awake and talking Mr. Flood's exacerbation ate him. He lay in the bed as if he were the death mask for someone underneath him. There was no motion to his body, his vital signs depressed to where he looked like a corpse, and the only things that moved at all were the little bubbles that ran every now and again to the top of the fluid in the I.V. bottle. They looked as if they were running out of him. He stayed that way for several hours, and then for no apparent reason he suddenly sat straight up in bed, his eyes still closed, his arms loose and dangling. "Holy Jesus, I hurt!" he yelled, and then he lay back down like a mechanical toy.

In the evening his wife came to see him. She entered the room with Mrs. Marvin at her side, and she looked very much as if she were going to a viewing: Dumb and intensely melancholy. She stood at the end of the bed, one arm interlocked with Mrs. Marvin's, and she looked down at her husband. "Bernie?" she said softly. There was no doubt from her tone that she did not want him to hear. "Bernie," she said again with much greater distance. She turned to Mrs. Marvin and said, "When is he going to die?"

"My dear," Mrs. Marvin said.

"Are there lots of others like him?" Mrs. Flood asked.

"A hospital is a place for people to get well," Mrs. Marvin said.

Mr. Flood shifted in his unconsciousness and his wife gave a sudden start and backed away from the bed. "Do you want me to get the cake now?" Mrs. Mavin asked. Mrs. Flood nodded and untangled her arm from Mrs. Marvin's. "His mother was so insistent," Mrs. Flood said as Mrs. Marvin left the room. Mrs. Flood moved around from the end of the bed and up toward the night table. She turned for a moment and looked at Mr. Miller and quietly said to herself, "You awful old person." Then she turned back to her husband and began a soft dribble of words, like rain that runs out a gutter after a shower has passed. "You should see her, Bernie," she said, unbuttoning her coat, "just as demanding as ever. Insisted you have your favorite, the chocolate layer cake you liked as a boy. She was up half the night making it. Her eyes are weaker now, you know. She had to read that old recipe through a magnifying glass." Mrs. Marvin came in carrying a Spode plate with a large metal food warmer over it. She set it down on the night table and Mrs. Flood looked at it. "He so loves his mother's cakes," she said to Mrs. Marvin, and together they turned and left the room.

By the middle of the next afternoon the exacerbations were running out, but both men were weaker than ever before. Their sicknesses this time had been short but very intense, and they lay in their beds bewildered by their own weakness, the very act of breathing exhausting. "Flood?" Mr. Miller said. "Are you there?" He could not turn his head to see.

"I guess so," Mr. Flood said. When he turned his eyes all he could see was the plastic tube that ran from his arm to the

Going Gently

empty bottle on the I.V. pole. Some blood from his arm had backed up several feet into the empty tube, but for some reason Mr. Flood took no notice of it.

The men were very quiet and motionless for a long time. Each seemed more forced into himself than before, and each feared that he was much sicker than the other. Finally, Mr. Flood said, "I really didn't believe it before. It was like maybe I was going to be really sick for a long time but then I'd get well. I don't believe that any more."

"Do you think they'll feed us tonight?" Mr. Miller said. But when he got no response he knew that Mr. Flood had fallen into a quick, shallow sleep. He lay looking at the ceiling cracks the painters had failed to fill, and then he remembered the day before when the young nurse had been in the room and he had forgotten what he wanted to say to her. In a kind of private interior panic he began to try to remember things form his past: Address numbers of apartments and houses, his Social Security number, a telephone number, any telephone number, dates, amounts on paychecks. None of them came to him and his panic increased. His right hand came up to rub his forehead and it came away moist with sweat. But then, almost on command from someone unseen, Mr. Miller began to speak softly. What he said to himself in so spontaneous a way that he was unaware of it was all the things he had taught so often that he knew them by heart. Poems and passages from novels came verbatim from him and it was as though his mind were turning the pages of some great anthology. He went on reciting, or, rather, reading to himself for almost an hour before he realized what he was doing. Finally he said to his disease, "Not my brain, you bastard. That you don't get."

The men did receive dinner that evening, but they had to be fed, Mr. Miller by the young nurse, Mr. Flood by the orderly. The conversations that took place, one between Mr. Miller and Mr. Flood, the other between the nurse and the orderly, were very much like a bridge that carries traffic on two separate levels—neither aware of the other. The nurse and orderly talked to each other about a staff party they had heard about where two interns had been arrested, and Mr. Miller and Mr. Flood took note of their presence only when the food hung out before their mouths while some juicy detail of the party was minutely described. Then one of the men would break into the description to get his food. When the nurse and the orderly finished feeding the men they wiped their faces for them and brought small pans of water for their hands, which were still clean.

As Mr. Miller rolled slightly in his bed to set the pan on the night table he saw the cake. "What's that, Flood?" he said. He balanced for a moment on one elbow. Mr. Flood rolled over a little and looked at the plate and then he told Mr. Miller he hadn't any idea what it was. Then, with some excitement in his voice, he said, "It's from my mother. I know the plate."

"Can you reach it?" Mr. Miller asked.

"No."

"What do you think it is?"

"Something to eat," Mr. Flood said. "Whenever she made me something to eat she always put it on that plate."

"Cherries jubilee," Mr. Miller said, and he collapsed down from his elbow position.

"It's probably a cake, probably a chocolate cake."

"Just what you need," Mr. Miller said.

"I bet my wife brought it," Mr. Flood said.

"Shall we ring for the nurse and have her serve it up?" Mr. Miller asked.

"Let it go," Mr. Flood said. "Maybe tomorrow."

"Did it occur to you that I might want some of it?"

"No," Mr. Flood said. "Do you?"

"Not on your life."

After a few minutes the men sank into twilight sleeps where all they were aware of was the dead yellow color behind their closed eyelids. Every now and again Mr. Flood would make a little cry when some part of him hurt, but that was all.

Mr. Miller was the first to awaken, and when he did he saw

Going Gently

Mr. Flood's son standing in the middle of the room. "Hello," Mr. Miller said to him.

"Is my father awake?" the son asked.

"Yes," Mr. Flood answered for himself.

"Mother couldn't come. She's got sinus again," the young man said.

"Where have you been?" Mr. Flood said like a command. "The shop's been frantic."

"You making good money?"

"Oceans."

"How come you can't take an hour off to come and see me?"

"It's been gruesome," the son said. "We've had the most fantastic sales. Bells are going out faster than they came in. There's hardly a way to keep up."

"Is your mother sleeping okay?"

"I made her keep her door open and she's promised that if she has trouble she'll come right in and wake me up. And she's got some new red pills. They help her enormously." He kept talking simply to keep his mouth moving and he watched his father close his eyes and drift off to sleep again. He stood for a moment and then turned to Mr. Miller. "Is he sleeping a lot like this?"

"No."

"How are you feeling?"

"Rotten, like your father."

"It's such a shame," the son said. He appeared to rise very close to the point of tears.

"It certainly is."

"The strain on us, on Mother."

"You're an ass," Mr. Miller said. "A perfect ass. But you know you are."

"You haven't any right to say that."

"Every right in the world, young man," Mr. Miller said. His voice was suddenly quite strong. "You don't care about your father. You don't want it to be over for him, you want it to be over for you."

Going Gently

"You self centered sadist," the young man said.

"Beat it," Mr. Miller said, and Mr. Flood's son turned and left the room without looking at his father.

"I heard that," Mr. Flood said.

"Well, I'm sorry if you did," Mr. Miller answered.

"There's always been something," Mr. Flood said, "and I'm going to feel like garbage for saying it, but there's always been something about him I never liked. I guess you shouldn't say that about your kid."

"Absolutely not," Mr. Miller said.

Then, after a long pause, Mr. Flood said loudly, "What I'd like is for someone, anyone, to come in here and say, 'Well, you're dying, you poor son of a bitch, but you're still a human being, you still wake up every now and again in the morning and think about women.'"

FOUR

The next morning the men were somehow different, somehow drawn more into their beds. The room seemed as if it had been divided into two separate isolation chambers. The men did not speak to each other until the breakfast trays came, and when they saw the same food on the same trays they toyed with it without appetite, without feeling. Neither even looked at the other for a very long time. Finally Mr. Flood said, "Do you feel cold?"

"I do."

"Is it the room?"

"It's metabolism."

"You know," Mr. Flood said, and he rolled back one of the sleeves on his robe, "I don't think I've got a real muscle left anywhere. There's just a kind of gnawing, not pain, not real pain. Just a kind of long ache I can't pin down."

"Tell that to them when they make their rounds," Mr. Miller said.

Going Gently

"*Ha,*" Mr. Flood said. "Those cheesy bastards don't give a damn what you tell them."

"Tell them anyway," Mr. Miller answered. "I'm off duty." He pushed his tray from him and lay back as if he were going to settle down on a bed of nails.

"What's got you this morning?"

"Sometimes I simply do not wish to talk. Is that so difficult for you to understand?"

"But I want to talk."

"Then ring for one of the merciful white mannequins and talk her to death. You're paying forty-seven whatever for that privilege."

"I want to talk to you."

"And I want to be left alone."

"Too damn bad," Mr. Flood said. "If I want to talk to you, I will."

"Then talk," Mr. Miller said. He lay on the bed perfectly immobile as Mr. Flood began to speak in random phrases and disconnected thoughts.

"It's like, well, like I feel maybe I'm too heavy to carry around any more. You know what I mean? It's getting lighter and heavier all at the same time. You feel like that?"

"More or less."

"Tell me how you feel," Mr. Flood said. There was a warm, almost urgent tone in his voice.

"I can't tell you how I feel," Mr. Miller began softly. "No more than I can get rid of how I feel." He coughed a low, long bubble that stayed deep in his chest. "But if you want me to talk," he said, "I'll tell you something I don't much like—and it was nowhere in the reading I've done. I think this thing does more damage to your spirit than to your body."

"Jesus, but I see red sometimes," Mr. Flood said.

"You're most fortunate," Mr. Miller answered. "All the books I've read say that getting angry is the best thing. I'm afraid, however, that is not in my repertoire of counterattack. As a matter of fact, I am convinced that my repertoire is

Going Gently

finally depleted. Now will you please shut your mouth and leave me alone?" He turned on his side and first faced the wall, then slowly drew his knees toward his chest as if for protection.

A little while later two residents and Miss Scarli came into the room for morning rounds. Mr. Flood was sitting up in bed; Mr. Miller was still in his fetal position. The two doctors went first to Mr. Flood. Simultaneously they said good morning to him, and he looked from one to the other and then to Miss Scarli. She turned to look at Mr. Miller. "Remove your robe, please," one of the doctors said to Mr. Flood. He did so with considerable effort. Miss Scarli had to help him off with the sleeves. After he removed the gown he realized that one of the doctors was explaining his condition to the other. He looked to each of the men in front of him, but he was unable to catch the eye of either, and after a while he fixed his gaze beyond them on a long, sloppy drip line the painters had left. He felt the doctors examine him as if he were momentarily to be placed on auction, and they were very thorough with him. There was talk of muscle tonus, of biopsies, appetite, autonomic disfunction, and then Mr. Flood completely tuned them out. He did not realize that the younger of the two doctors was speaking to him until he had been asked for the third time how he felt. Mr. Flood's eyes slowly came in on the young man and he said, "Do you really want to know?" The doctor said he did. "I don't feel," Mr. Flood said. "I don't feel nothing."

"Where?"

"Everywhere," Mr. Flood answered. "Nothing everywhere."

"Do you have significant discomfort?"

"No," Mr. Flood said.

The doctor took the chart from Miss Scarli and glanced at it. "You have diarrhea," he said as if he were the first to make the discovery.

"Want some?" Mr. Flood said.

"I am trying to help you," the doctor said.

"My ass," Mr. Flood said.

"We *are* trying to help you," the older doctor put in.

"La de da," Mr. Flood said. "You guys aren't going to help anyone. Your problem is you're stuck with us. Plain stuck and there ain't a thing in God's sweet kingdom you can do. Why make out like you're trying, like you got some hot-titty formula up your sleeve waiting to try on me?"

"Research is constantly proceeding," Mr. Miller called out.

"On rats," Mr. Flood said.

"We do not have to tolerate this kind of behavior," the older doctor said.

"I know that," Mr. Flood said. He struggled back into his gown and let it hang loosely from his shoulders. The three people turned away from him as if they were leaving a store window.

As if in anticipation Mr. Miller began to roll away from the wall to face them. "Homer," Miss Scarli said, "you look awful." The two doctors looked at her with expressions that showed they were clearly surprised by her familiarity. As she backed away Mr. Miller said, "Quite right, Scarli." Then to the doctors, "What do you want from me?"

They said nothing and quickly went to work on him as if he were a model they were trying to assemble. They stripped his robe from him and then pulled his gown down to his waist, where it lay across his middle in white cotton rolls. The older doctor placed his stethoscope in various positions on Mr. Miller's chest, somewhat as if he were playing a fast game of checkers, and when he came near the diaphragm he motioned to the other doctor to listen along with him. They stayed in their awkward positions for a long time, only occasionally moving their stethoscopes a few inches. Finally, as the men raised up, Mr. Miller said, "Are you going to drain me?"

"I think it's time," the older doctor said. "It'll take the pressure off for a while." He helped Mr. Miller to sit as erect as he could, and then he took a small pencil flashlight from his lapel pocket and began to examine Mr. Miller's eyes.

"What are you looking for?" Mr. Miller asked.

"How much do you drink?" the doctor asked.

"I don't know. A manageable amount," Mr. Miller said.

The doctor eased him back to the horizontal and told him to suck in a deep breath, and then, with both hands held flat and together so that they seemed to Mr. Miller to form the head of a spear, the doctor pressed hard and deep into the area just below the diaphragm. He rolled his fingertips back and forth and Mr. Miller gasped. The doctor popped his fingers out and said, "I'd advise you to stop drinking."

"Oh, really?"

"There's a noticeable hardening about several lobes of your liver," he said. "And your sclera are questionable for jaundice."

"How long would you estimate my liver has?"

"I don't know," the doctor said, "but the continuance of alcohol will not help it any."

"You really must try to stop drinking so much," Miss Scarli put in.

"If you start acting like a withered old hen, I shall be very disappointed in you," Mr. Miller said. "Now, as for you two goons, I would appreciate it if you would zip shut the advice machine you anatomically refer to as a mouth."

"Did you know that teachers have one of the highest indices of alcoholism among professional groups?" the young doctor said.

Mr. Miller slowly looked the young doctor up and down and then said to him, "No, you don't say."

"The results of that particular study are fascinating," the doctor said. Mr. Miller saw Miss Scarli look at the doctor and then drop her head in pure embarrassment.

"Let me tell you something, young man," Mr. Miller said, "and I hope you'll remember it at least until you're old enough to understand it. I drink," he said and then paused, "and I shall continue to drink because, when I don't, life is very simply sitting in a painfully small room with two T.V.'s, three stereo F.M. broadcasts, and six baritone lady bridge players." The young doctor's eyes were growing wide. "And here's another thing while I'm at it," he went on. "There are the likes of you, mummified low-echelon scientists, who have never had a sensitive nerve in your head touched. You are the luckiest people who ever walked the earth. You *are* the chosen. Your vision of life is to be envied, your ability to sleep eight straight hours studied and emulated. But you are fools made of stone."

"For God's sake, shut him up," Mr. Flood said. "Do something to shut him up."

But from the way the doctors conducted themselves it was clear that they had not really heard Mr. Miller. And Miss Scarli, who had left the room just as Mr. Miller was beginning to speak, had already returned with the instruments for the thoracentesis. Mr. Miller continued to sit on the edge of the bed like a soggy piece of fruit. He did not seem to be aware any longer of the people who worked around him. He sat staring toward the open door. The young doctor took the hypodermic needle with the local anesthetic in it and injected it into Mr. Miller's left side between the fourth and fifth ribs. Then he stepped to one side and the older doctor put an eight-inch needle on the end of a large empty syringe. He placed it between Mr. Miller's ribs and with a quick, rude gesture thrust it into his chest. Mr. Miller looked down at the long needle and watched it disappear into his side. After a few moments the doctor began to draw out bloody red fluid from his chest. He filled the large syringe, unscrewed it from the needle and handed it to Miss Scarli. She gave the doctor an empty one and he put it back on the needle and filled it. "A hundred c.c.'s," he said to Miss Scarli as he took that syringe off the needle. But when he started to fill the third syringe he saw that the fluid from Mr. Miller's side had become clear and watery. The doctor did not pull on the end of the syringe to get the fluid out. He simply held the syringe and let the slightly pumping fluid fill it. Then he extracted the needle. A clear bubble formed for a moment over the small hole in Mr. Miller's side, and then it ran slowly down over the next two ribs. "Now take a deep breath," the doctor said to Mr. Miller.

Going Gently

He did so and smiled faintly at the feeling of emptiness in his left side. "Much relief," he said.

"We'll do the other side tomorrow," the doctor said.

They put him down gently on his bed and he turned to lie on his right side. For the first time in many days he breathed easily.

When the doctors and Miss Scarli left the room it was as if the lights had been dimmed. There was a pall, a feeling about the place that both men sensed. Stale odors seemed to slide down from the walls like remnants of dead ceremonies. Both men looked and felt much smaller in their beds, and for the first time it seemed as if neither cared about the other. Mr. Miller rolled over and stared into the center of the room, his eyes moving quickly from one square of linoleum to another, and Mr. Flood looked past the foot of Mr. Miller's bed to the window. From his angle in bed all he could see was a metallic rectangle of sky, but his eyes stayed there wide and unblinking.

They lay where they were for a long time, each looking as if he were sound asleep except for his eyes. There was a limp, dead quality to their bodies, the kind of total immobility that comes with deep sleep, but their eyes remained fixed as if on personal objects of horror.

They stayed that way for most of the day, and even during meals there was no communication between them. Miss Scarli came into the room during lunch to ask the men how they were. Mr. Miller did not even look up when he told her to go away. She turned to Mr. Flood and asked him how he was. He shook his head as if disgusted and Miss Scarli left the room. When the men had finished the meal they lay back again on their beds and resumed staring.

But near the end of the afternoon Mr. Flood was jarred out of his depression by the sounds of Mr. Miller's crying. The sounds came into Mr. Flood's consciousness slowly, as from a great distance, and when he moved his head on the pillow to look at Mr. Miller he had to concentrate to focus his eyes.

Going Gently

"You okay?" Mr. Flood asked, but his voice was so soft that it did not carry to the other bed. "What's wrong?" he said, but there was no answer. Mr. Flood tried to shift on his bed, but his body was stiff from remaining stationary so long. "Mr. Miller, you all right?" Mr. Flood finally said loud enough to be heard.

"I've never been better," Mr. Miller said.

"Why are you crying?"

"Shut up."

"You got pain?"

"No."

"If they find you crying, they're going to get worried."

"They have seen people cry before."

Mr. Flood very slowly sat up a little in bed. "Is there something I can get you?" he asked.

"No," Mr. Miller said.

"You sure you ain't got pain?"

"I have done this with varying regularity for several months now," Mr. Miller said. He wiped his eyes with his sleeve. "It seems in the long run to make me feel better."

"So you ain't so tough?"

"Jerk."

"That's more like it," Mr. Flood said.

"I mean that."

"Sure, sure."

"You are a consummate fool," Mr. Miller said.

"I know, I know."

"Do you have the remotest idea why I am crying?" Mr. Miller said.

"You're afraid," Mr. Flood said.

"Does the student turn teacher now?" Mr. Miller said.

"You're scared to death."

"Maybe so," Mr. Miller said to him. "But I am not afraid of being dead, only dying."

"What's the difference?"

"You are a poor, sad fool," Mr. Miller said.

"That's more like it."

89

Going Gently

"Damn you, Flood, shut up," Mr. Miller said viciously. "Get one thing straight in your head. I don't want anything from you, nothing any more from anybody."

"You can't just go and give up," Mr. Flood said as if he were reading it in a book.

"You just watch," Mr. Miller said. He rolled to his back. "I want the miserable goddamn thing done with," he said. He put a forearm across his eyes. "*Me, me*. Not another thing counts. Nothing. I am tired of this room, of you, of Scarli, of these dribbling fools who stick me in the side, of just plain waking up in the morning." He rolled his head out from under his arm and said, "You disgust me, Flood. You are a stupid man and you disgust me."

"You son of a bitch," Mr. Flood said. "I've had enough out of you." He tried to raise himself further in the bed but he could not. "I don't have to take nothing from you. Who the hell says you count? How the Christ you think I feel?"

"I couldn't care less," Mr. Miller said.

"That goes double."

"Witty," Mr. Miller said. "And just what is it, may I ask, that you've done with your life that gives you the right to lie there and tell me I shouldn't feel like my soul is a spittoon?"

"I done a hell of a lot more than you," he answered quickly. "For one thing, I worked. And I worked damn hard."

"If I could get my hands across my chest you would hear long and deserving applause."

"All you ever done was to sit on your ass."

"And talk," Mr. Miller added.

"That's right," Mr. Flood said. "And what have you got to show for it? Nothing."

"Agreed," Mr. Miller said. "I do indeed have nothing to show for it. You, however, have a wife, a son, and money in the bank."

"Damned right I do," Mr. Flood said.

"Your wife barely knows you any more, your son is nothing

Going Gently

but a distant enemy. And eighteen thousand dollars at your age is hardly money in the bank."

"You can look at it any way you want."

The men slept into the early evening, Mr. Miller a solid, immovable lump in his bed, Mr. Flood slowly gyrating in a light sleep as if he were being tortured by dreams. When he awakened his face was wet with sweat and very red. He called out to Mr. Miller, but there was no answer. He tried to wake Mr. Miller several times, and when he couldn't he was seized by a sudden, hard panic. He pressed his call button and waited, but no one came. Finally he sat up quickly in bed with an ease that suggested his strength had suddenly been fully restored. He tied his robe across his middle and slid from the bed and stood trying to clear his head and master his balance. He called softly to Mr. Miller again, and when there was no answer he thought for a minute that Mr. Miller was dead. He steadied his gaze on Mr. Miller's back, and when the saw the slow stretching of the blue robe around his shoulders he knew that his breathing was steady. He looked around the room again and then he said out loud, "Oh, God, I got to talk to someone." He turned like a commuter leaving a late train and was gone from the room.

Mr. Miller awakened about half an hour later and called to Mr. Flood. When there was no answer he called again. Finally he rolled over, and when he saw the empty bed he was very frightened. His eyes swept the room time and again, and each time his gaze came to rest on Mr. Flood's bed he truly expected to find him there. Mr. Miller took the call button in his hand and began pressing it as if he were sending out a Mayday message. But when after a few moments no one came to the room Mr. Miller put down the call button and simply began to call Mr. Flood's name. It was almost as if he were tired of a game of hide and seek, and he seemed certain that if he only tried hard enough Mr. Flood would finally come out of the closet or from under the bed. After a few more minutes,

Going Gently

though, Mr. Miller stopped calling. He sat on the edge of the bed and stared at the floor.

When Mr. Flood did return to the room it was in a wheelchair being pushed by Mrs. Marvin. Mr. Flood's face was flushed and he had the leering, happy expression of a Saturday night drunk. "You are responsible for this," Mrs. Marvin said to Mr. Miller.

"I've done nothing," Mr. Miller said. He was looking at Mr. Flood.

"You wouldn't wake up," Mr. Flood said to him. "I needed to talk to you."

Mrs. Marvin helped Mr. Flood get back into bed in a manner that suggested she had once loaded laundry trucks, and then she turned to Mr. Miller and said, "My patience with you has just about run out."

"Come any closer and I'll bite you," Mr. Miller said. He had not taken his eyes from Mr. Flood, and when Mrs. Marvin left the room he said to him, "This had better be good, Flood."

"I had to talk, see?" Mr. Flood said. His breathing was light and fast, but he had no difficulty laughing. "It's crazy out there," he said. "The halls are loaded with people. Visitors, nurses, doctors, everybody under the sun is out there. All I wanted to do was talk to a couple of people. But nobody knew me. It was crazy. All those doctors and nursers and nobody knew me." He paused and took in some air. "I tried to stop this young nurse and she never even looked at me. She said, 'Excuse me,' and kept right on going. I could have been offering hundred-dollar bills and still have the whole wad. It's crazy out there. And I tried to stop a doctor and he looked at me and said I shouldn't be out of bed without my slippers."

"I think you're off your head," Mr. Miller said.

"Then I went up to a lady in a real nice fur coat and I just said hello to her. She told me to leave her alone and she busted out crying."

"You are off your head."

"Then I saw the phone booth," Mr. Flood went on. "If

Going Gently

there had been a seat in it, I'd still be there. My pins just gave out and that's when Marvin found me."
"Who'd you try to call?" Mr. Miller asked.
"Nobody."
"Did you call your home?"
"Yes," Mr. Flood said quietly.
"And there wasn't anybody there," Mr. Miller said.
"I'll bet they're on their way over," Mr. Flood said.
"How much?"
"About a nickel."

The mood of the room held on black through the night and into the next morning. Mr. Miller cried very hard toward midnight, but Mr. Flood did nothing about it. He cried again about six in the morning, but this time it was a softer, gentler thing, as if he were crying about some large, sad idea. Mr. Flood awakened and asked if Mr. Miller was all right, and when there was no answer he rolled over in his bed and went back to sleep.

When the breakfast trays came Mr. Miller never even turned over. Mr. Flood ate well for the first time in several days, and all the while he sat looking at Mr. Miller's back. Every now and again he said to Mr. Miller that he should try the eggs, or the juice, or that the tea seemed better than usual. Still there was no reaction from Mr. Miller. Finally Mr. Flood said, "What gives over there?"

"Get Scarli," Mr. Miller said very quietly.
"You okay?"
"Get her," Mr. Miller said again, and Mr. Flood pressed long and hard on his call button.

When she came into the room Mr. Flood pointed at Mr. Miller. "Homer?" Miss Scarli said very tentatively as she came toward his bed. He did not move. "Homer?" she said again. He moved his body slightly but he did not take his eyes from the wall. She leaned over him and said, "You look very bad."

"I am," he told her. "I've misjudged everything."

"How do you feel?" she asked. He knew from the tone of her voice that she truly wanted to know.

"Awkward," he said. "I know that doesn't help, but it's like everything is suddenly off center, tilted."

"Do you have pain?"

"The usual." He looked at Miss Scarli intensely and then he quickly added, "What's it like when it finally comes?"

"I don't have an answer," she said. "You know that."

"It's my guess it's an incredible numbing."

"Is that how you feel?"

"You're about the nicest person I ever met," Mr. Miller said.

"Not now, Homer," she said. "Tell me how you feel."

"Numb," he said. He looked away from her to his feet. He regarded them for a moment as if they were distant traffic signs.

"You could be getting worse," Miss Scarli told him.

"Remission chances nil?"

"No, not at all," she said. "It depends on you, on what you want."

"Are we finally down to where it's an act of will for me to live?" he said. "Am I now supposed to win one for the Gipper?"

"I'm not going to lie to you."

"You couldn't if your life depended on it."

"You're terribly sick," she said.

"Don't get emotional about it."

"You could die today, tomorrow, any time," she said flatly. "But whatever you do will only get you time."

"There's one thing wrong with your super-formula for living," he said. "Don't I have to have a reason, the will?"

"You sure do," she said.

"And what in the name of God shall that reason be?" he said. "A morbid desire to delay the inevitable? Effort, energy, pain expended and endured so that I might draw a few hundred thousand more breaths?"

"You can do whatever you want," she said.

"It's so goddamn easy for you to act tough," he said.

Going Gently

"That's exactly what all you patients wallowing in self-pity love to believe," she threw at him. "What you do is take and take from us. With never an iota of return, nothing. You think when we leave here in the afternoon we go home and down a six-pack with a half a pound of chocolates and wiggle our toes in front of some T.V. medical show, all the while saying how wonderful to be a nurse. B.S., buster. You want to die right now, you go ahead and do it. It's going to make tomorrow a hell of a lot easier on me." She turned to leave the room and Mr. Miller called softly to her to come back, but she did not.

"What did you do to her?" Mr. Flood asked.

"Oh, shut up."

"Come on, what'd you do?"

"If you don't shut up, I'm going to come over there and beat you into silence," Mr. Miller said.

"Miss Scarli really got to you, didn't she?" Mr. Flood said. His voice rippled sweetly like a little cup of Jell-O.

"If you must know, I told Scarli I felt like hell," Mr. Miller said.

"You're scared, too," Mr. Flood said.

"Why is it so important to you that I tell you I'm afraid?" Mr. Miller said.

"I don't know," Mr. Flood said. His head dropped down as if he were looking at a missing button on his front.

"You have been chattering like a schoolgirl."

"I don't understand nothing," Mr. Flood dribbled. His tone was one of total defeat. "I don't understand my Glad and my boy and all this mess." He looked to Mr. Miller and tears were riding freely down his cheeks. "I'm *not* an old man, damn it. I'm sixty-seven years old and everybody's written me off like I was a hundred and eight."

"I haven't written you off," Mr. Miller said quietly.

"You don't count. You ain't got nobody else, either."

"True enough," Mr. Miller said. "But I have thought what this would be like if your bed were empty, if they had stored me in a private room with a private bath and a private closet. Has that thought ever occurred to you?"

"Sure it has," Mr. Flood said.
"You would have been dead a week ago," Mr. Miller told him.
"It would have been better," Mr. Flood simpered on. "Anything would have been better than this." He looked down again to his chest and ran his hand over it and down to his belly. "You know that I weigh? You got any idea what I weigh?"
"Not very much," Mr. Miller said.
"A hundred and thirty-nine pounds," he said. His hand moved down onto his thighs. "When I came in here I was damn near one eighty." He slammed his fist down on the mattress and it made almost no sound.

For several hours the men lay in their beds as they had before, and they were distracted from themselves only by a stiff persistent wind they heard plainly. It whistled along the window and as it increased the light outside began to dim down. After another hour an orderly came into the room and went straight to the window to see if it was locked. "Looks like the tip of the hurricane's coming after all," he said. When the rain did come in a few more minutes it was like sonatas on the window. For a long time the men ignored the storm, but when a giant ball of wind flattened itself against the panes in a long rattle Mr. Flood slowly sat up in bed. "Jesus," he said. He tied his robe about him and looked toward the window. "What's it doing?" Mr. Miller asked.
"It looks like all hell's breaking loose," Mr. Flood said. He slid from the edge of the bed and shuffled toward the window. Mr. Miller turned to his back and propped himself up on his elbows. He watched Mr. Flood rub away the thin film of steam on the window and then look out. "Can you see from there?" Mr. Flood asked. Mr. Miller got out of bed with great difficulty, and very slowly, with one hand on the mattress, he moved toward the end of the bed. The men stood together and watched the rain and wind steadily strip the trees in front

Going Gently

of the hospital of their few final leaves. "It'd be a hell of a day for making calls," Mr. Flood said.

They stood shoulder to shoulder for a few minutes, and both stepped back a little as a great billow of wind pressed against the window and shook it. "Look," Mr. Flood said and half-raised his arm.

"I see it," Mr. Miller said. They watched a small stream of water rise out of one of the corners of a pane and run quickly down to the sill, where it divided into two, each going separately toward the floor. "Jesus, that's a wind," Mr. Flood said. "It shoved the water right through the window."

They stepped close to the window again and looked out just in time to see the wind bend a large oak tree in front of the hospital. It was a steady bending, a great bowing out of the trunk a third of the way up. All the branches were forced into the same direction and held there as if they had suddenly become marble. There was a great cracking sound that followed and the tree held its tension for only another second or two. It fell as if in slow motion across the empty sidewalk and into a parking space. When it was suddenly still the men saw where the trunk had split into two great pointed pieces.

Mr. Flood got very sick that afternoon. It came on him like a long, fast wave and he barely had time to collect his thoughts as the sickness swelled over him. Mr. Miller called for Miss Scarli, but another nurse came and said there was nothing they could do for Mr. Flood. All during the afternoon Mr. Flood eased in and out of consciousness so often that it was impossible for Mr. Miller to tell when he was awake. He had brought the straight-back chair next to Mr. Flood's bed and placed his book at the foot of the bed. He was leaning over reading from it when Mr. Flood awakened. "What are you doing out of bed?" Mr. Flood said to him.

"I'm feeling better," Mr. Miller said without looking up from the book.

"No, you aren't," Mr. Flood said.

"I am," Mr. Miller said. He turned a page.

"I think I know how you been feeling the last couple of days," Mr. Flood said.

"Rotten," Mr. Miller said.

Mr. Flood nodded slightly and then said, "What are you reading?" His voice was light and fast but there was no tension in it.

"What do you think I'm reading?"

"Knowing you, probably a book on embalming."

"Nonsense," Mr. Miller said. "I haven't the slightest interest in what they do to me when I'm dead. I'm reading, if you must know, about what this book calls the 'final stages.' Never in all my life have I been so disappointed. This tome is some seven hundred-odd pages and these asinine authorities have devoted all of eighteen pages to what they call the 'terminal phase.' If this were a student paper, God forbid, I should give it an F for outlandish vagueness."

"What's it doing out?" Mr. Flood asked.

"It hasn't let up a bit."

"Will you do something for me?" Mr. Flood suddenly blurted.

"What?" Mr. Miller said. He looked to Mr Flood with all his attention.

"If my family comes tonight and I'm asleep," he said. Then he pressed on quickly as if he had rehearsed it. "Would you tell them I don't want them to come any more?"

"I will not," Mr. Miller answered.

"Please?"

"The answer is an emphatic no," Mr. Miller said.

"Why?" Mr. Flood whined.

"It's none of my business," Mr. Miller said quietly. He turned several more pages.

"I really don't feel so good," Mr. Flood said. He rolled his head to one side. "I just don't want to see them no more."

"I should doubt very much if they wanted to see you," Mr. Miller said.

"We was never very close," Mr. Flood said. His eyes were pinned to the floor.

Going Gently

"It isn't that, Flood."

"Then what?"

"Your consistent inability to observe the obvious is tedious."

"You really think you're a big deal with your words."

"I do," Mr. Miller said. He flipped shut the book. "In fact, there has not been an idea in my head in twenty-odd years that hasn't received expression commensurate with its degree of profundity."

"Words is all you ever had," Mr. Flood said.

"And now you need them," Mr. Miller said. "You want me to use them for you. I shall not be your spokesman to your family, Flood. No more than I will go before the Almighty to plead for your marginal deliverance."

"But what do I say to them?" Mr. Flood asked.

"Why don't you want them to come?"

"I want it as easy on me as I can get it," Mr. Flood said.

"You don't have to tell them any more than that," Mr. Miller said.

"They want that, don't they?" Mr. Flood said. He brought his eyes to Mr. Miller's. "They want it easy on me."

"It would be foolish to ignore the reality that they also want it easy on themselves."

It was easy for everybody. Mr. Flood's wife and son did come that evening and they were very proud of having done so, as Mrs. Flood said, with the weather as inhuman as it was. It was easy on Mr. Flood because his wife and son did not even remove their coats. They unbuttoned them and flipped the lapels free of water, but they did not take them off. His son stood at the foot of the bed trying to fix the catch on his umbrella, and his wife made no attempt to hide the fact that she wanted praise for having come to the hospital. When Mrs. Flood asked him how he felt he told her that he wasn't very good, that he had had a difficult time during the past two days. "The lawyer is going to bring some things," she said. Then she stood looking past him toward the wall. Finally Mr.

Going Gently

Flood said that he did not want them to come any more, and his wife told him that she thought it would be best that way. She patted his upper arm once, and then again as though to verify that it was so bony. Then she turned quickly and as she passed the foot of the bed she took her son's arm and turned him toward the hall. He pivoted, his eyes and hands fascinated by the umbrella, and went with his mother.

There was a very long silence in the room until Mr. Flood finally said to Mr. Miller, "Will you call me Bernie?"

"I shall do nothing of the sort," Mr. Miller said to him. "And if you start getting sentimental I shall sue you for divorce."

The storm held on for several hours, rising and falling against the window. The men lay in their beds and listened to the rain run against the window first in giant spatters and then in rippling waves like piano music. It seemed for a while as if it were a third person trying to get in the room. But the storm began to blow itself out along about eleven, just when the hall lights were turned out and the men could see only two soft yellow lights from the baseboard in the hall. Their sleeping pills lay in tiny cups on their night tables, and as Mr. Miller turned in his bed to take his Mr. Flood said, "What are you thinking about?"

"Same thing you are."

"You got any whisky left?"

"You're not up to it," Mr. Miller said.

"You could bring me some."

"Take your pill," Mr. Miller said.

"I want a drink."

"All right, all right," Mr. Miller answered. Very slowly he put his robe around him, tied it and painfully got out of bed. He stood for a few seconds with both hands behind him on the edge of the mattress. He took a half-full bottle of whisky from the cabinet of the night table and went to Mr. Flood's bed. "With water or without?" he said.

"Just a little, with a lot of water," Mr. Flood said. Mr.

Miller poured the whisky and added the water. He poured only a very little for himself and sat in the chair. Mr. Miller looked at Mr. Flood for a long time. Finally Mr. Flood said, "How long you think you got?"

"A week, more or less."

"Me?"

"The same, more or less."

"It doesn't bother me so much, you know," Mr. Flood said.

"Yes, it does."

"But not like before. For some reason it just ain't like it was. Don't ask me why." Mr. Flood took a very small sip from the glass. He winced at the bitter taste and set the glass down on the night table.

"It says in here," Mr. Miller said, and he tapped the book, "that sooner or later we will inevitably accept."

"Do you?"

"Hardly in the way this compendium of idiocy suggests," Mr. Miller said. He sipped from his glass and then looked back to Mr. Flood. "Do you mind if I say something profound?"

"If you got to."

"The thing is somehow to keep moving, to keep on going on."

"That's accepting it," Mr. Flood said.

Mr. Miller put his hand around Mr. Flood's ankle and held it for a moment. "Not really," he said.

FIVE

The morning broke into the room with a clear yellow sun. The rays were neither direct nor warm. They slanted harshly through the window and cut an acute angle between the beds. It was the kind of sun that looked summery and strong, but there was very little about it that was pleasant except its color. For all of its apparent brightness, it did not even begin to flush out the darker corners of the room.

Mr. Miller did not awaken until his breakfast tray was put on his table, and when he turned over he saw that Mr. Flood was already eating. "Is it the usual?" he asked without looking at his tray.

"I got an extra box of cereal from Miss Scarli," Mr. Flood said. He held up a small box of Rice Krispies.

"Perfectly thrilling," Mr. Miller said.

"You feeling okay this morning?" Mr. Flood asked. His voice was low and testing.

"I am adequate," Mr. Miller said. He pulled his sheet back and slowly sat up. He put his legs over the side of the bed and

Going Gently

pulled his tray toward him. He sat looking at the tray, then he lifted the metal covering from the plate and put his index finger into the middle of a pile of scrambled eggs. "Unspeakably cold," he said. He reached out for the call button and was just about to press it when Miss Scarli came into the room. "You anticipate my every wish," he said to her.

"I know the eggs are cold," she said. "Everybody's eggs on the whole damn floor are cold."

"Mine were all right," Mr. Flood said. He looked down to his plate. Miss Scarli came across the room to Mr. Miller and put an individual-sized container of Rice Krispies on his tray.

"The warming ovens are out," she said.

"I detest cold cereal," Mr. Miller said.

"Detest it all you like," she answered. "It's all they've got left down there." She kept her eyes on his face as if she were looking for something.

"You could make us some toast," Mr. Miller said.

"I could make you eggs Benedict," she answered, "if I didn't have a whole floor going hungry."

"What are you going to do without me?" Mr. Miller said. He saw her smile as she went for the door. "Scarli is ninety-eight percent nurse and two percent woman," Mr. Miller said to Mr. Flood.

"Huh?" Mr. Flood said, and as he looked up several kernels of Rice Krispies dropped from his lips.

"When did you get your appetite back?"

"I'm hungry," Mr. Flood said. Mr. Miller took the small container of cereal and tossed it to Mr. Flood. "Thanks," Mr. Flood said. He split the box down the middle with his knife and dumped the cereal into his bowl. He began to eat with an almost insane intensity. Mr. Miller watched him for some time.

"You know what you're doing, don't you?" he finally said.

"No," Mr. Flood answered. He did not look up.

"You're feeding your disease."

"Drop dead," Mr. Flood said, and in two more spoonfuls he was done with it. "You never change, do you?" Mr. Flood said. He wiped his mouth and a little milk and cereal from the front of his robe. "Why do you say things like I'm feeding my disease?"

"It's there in the book," Mr. Miller said.

"I don't want to hear any more about that book." Mr. Flood's anger was barely under control.

"You are anti-intellectual," Mr. Miller said.

"The damn book wasn't written for me, you know. From now on you keep your little gems to yourself."

"The one thing about you I cannot figure out is why you are so set against the acquisition of knowledge," Mr. Miller said. He put both elbows on the table in front of him and held his head.

"What you like is getting things in your head you ain't never going to use."

Mr. Miller was looking down at his tray as though he had a set of lecture notes on it. When he looked up he saw Miss Scarli come through the door with a young minister whom Mr. Miller recognized immediately. "My, my," he said. The young minister looked at Mr. Miller as if he were viewing the face of sin itself. "This time I have come to see Mr. Flood," he said.

"Did you send for this creature?" Mr. Miller said to Mr. Flood. Mr. Flood looked from Mr. Miller to Miss Scarli and finally to the minister. "Well, Flood?" Mr. Miller prodded.

"Shut up, Homer," Miss Scarli said. "It's none of your business."

"Before you embrace this man's counseling," Mr. Miller said, "you should know that he will not argue very capably for the existence of a God." He looked to the young minister, whose blond crew cut framed his face from ear to ear like a nun's habit. "Nor does he even know the basic structure of the pure Calvinist sermon."

"Homer," Miss Scarli said softly.

"It's all right," the minister said.

"Of course it's all right," Mr. Miller said to Miss Scarli.

Going Gently

"The prerequisite for a bachelor's degree in divinity is a long and happy history of masochism."

"You are not a happy man," the minister said.

"Divinity is also a fudge," Mr. Miller said. He half-rolled back on his bed and then quickly turned to face the wall. The minister looked at Mr. Miller's form for a long moment and then turned like a motorized statue and looked at Mr. Flood.

"How are you?" he said slowly.

Mr. Flood brought his eyes from Mr. Miller to the young man and looked at him with an expression of thorough bewilderment. "What do you want?" he finally said.

"To talk to you," the minster said quietly.

"About what?" came the flat, dull response.

"I've spoken to your wife," he said, and then his voice trailed off as he watched Mr. Flood's gaze go back to Mr. Miller. But then he went on quickly. "Her concern is very great for you. She asked me to make certain that you have all you need."

"I'm okay," Mr. Flood said.

"Is there anything I can get you?"

"I don't need nothing."

"Is there anything," the young man began, and he stepped closer to the bed, "is there anything you'd like to tell me?"

"Make a clean breast of it, Flood," Mr. Miller called from his bed. The minister glanced at Mr. Miller, then his eyes came down hard on Mr. Flood like a detective about to solve some super-mystery.

"Yes?" he said to Mr. Flood.

"Yes, what?" Mr. Flood said.

"Tell him about the inhuman way you treated that cripple," Mr. Miller said. "At least get that one off your chest." The minster eased even closer.

"What are you talking about?" Mr. Flood said. He had to peek around the side of the minister to see Mr. Miller.

"I've done a lot for you, Flood," Mr. Miller said. "But I draw the line at surrogate confessor."

Going Gently

"What did you do to the cripple?" the minister asked Mr. Flood.

"Back off, will you?" Mr. Flood said. He raised his hand and the minister stepped back a little. Then he said across the room, "Mr. Miller, what the hell are you talking about?"

Mr. Miller rolled slowly to the middle of the bed, paused for a moment to gather strength, and then rolled onto his left side. "Surely you remember what you confided in me." Mr. Flood stared at Mr. Miller with a look that was totally blank. Mr. Miller propped himself on his left elbow and said to the minister, "What Flood did was to pass a crippled beggar who was selling pencils, you see, and next to the pencils was an empty hat. Flood went and put a quarter in the hat and when the cripple offered him a pencil Flood magnanimously refused it."

"I never did that," Mr. Flood said.

"The problem, of course, is obvious," Mr. Miller went on. "Was Flood's act of charity negated by his odorous self-righteousness in not taking the pencil? It would, you see, have been a more perfect act of charity to have taken the pencil."

"What's he talking about?" Mr. Flood said to Miss Scarli.

The minister was wrapped in concentration. "I wouldn't look at it that way at all," he said to Mr. Miller. "Like all things, it has to do with viewpoint."

"Had I been that beggar, I'd have thrown the quarter back in his face," Mr. Miller said.

"It would seem to me that the act of charity would in God's eyes stand alone. It would perhaps cancel the self-righteousness."

"Are you saying, then, that God is an accountant?" Mr. Miller asked.

"I am contending that there has to be discernible logic," the minister said.

"Flood, did you hear that?" Mr. Miller said.

"You're nutty as a fruitcake," Mr. Flood told him.

"The man said God is logical." Mr. Miller looked back to

the minister and said, "The implications of that remark are awesome, stupidly awesome. Your implication is that there is reason behind the two of us lying on these beds. You will never persuade me of that. Your training has been ludicrous, parochial. You have been trained to look down on situations instead of up to them." Quite suddenly it was clear that Mr. Miller's strength was fast draining from him. It was clear, too, that he was aware of it. His voice started to fade like a weak radio signal. He raised his right arm from the bed and pointed at the minister. His mouth opened as if it had suddenly become unhinged and then he fell back on the bed in exhaustion, Miss Scarli stepped past the minister and went to Mr. Miller. She bent over him and said, "That's enough." He half-smiled up at her. "Honest to God, Homer, I don't know what keeps you going sometimes."

"Get him out of here," he said to her quietly.

"He's got to do his job," Miss Scarli said.

Mr. Miller started to raise himself up, his face twisting into an almost evil determination, but when Miss Scarli put a hand on his shoulder he collapsed like a house of cards. "Homer," she said quietly, "why do you fight so hard for Mr. Flood? You don't even like him very much."

"I don't like him at all," Mr. Miller said. "He's a boor."

"Then why?"

"You're next," he said through his teeth.

Miss Scarli left the room with the minister in a way that suggested she was late for a train and he was her luggage. She told him that his time was up, hooked an arm through his and went out the door. Mr. Flood sat on his bed stupidly, as if he were waiting for a sentence to be completed. "Jesus, damn," he said, "what's going on? He wasn't such a bad guy."

"Do you need him?" Mr. Miller said softly.

"I only said he wasn't such a bad guy."

Mr. Miller started to answer him, but the sounds he tried to make tripped over the little bubbles of phlegm in his throat. He coughed in a spastic way, as if he had no idea it was coming, and his head cocked forward sharply. His nostrils flared as he tried hard to control his chest and still get some air down his tubes. But it didn't work. He coughed in a long, low rumble, and each time he tried to take a breath the coughing ran more ahead of him until there was no air left in his chest. "You all right?" Mr. Flood said. Mr. Miller came up on his elbows and managed to get a bit of air. Instantly he coughed that out and sucked in another little ration. He sat up more and finally got his legs over the side of the bed. He pointed to the metal kidney pan and his fingers danced in frustration as if they would speak for him. Mr. Flood got out of bed and, balancing himself first on his night table and then on Mr. Miller's reached the pan and handed it to him. He watched as Mr. Miller began to cough with the singular purpose of emptying his lungs. Slowly he got control of his breathing, and his coughing began to work for him. Mr. Flood leaned against the mattress and every now and again he reached around and gently slapped Mr. Miller on the back. Mr. Miller held the metal pan close to his mouth with his face bent over it. The pan began to fill with the stuff from his lungs and the water that ran freely from his nose and eyes. In the next few minutes Mr. Miller very slowly gathered his breathing under control enough so that he was able to swear softly under his breath. Then he raised the pan slightly and said thanks to Mr. Flood. "You want me to get somebody?" Mr. Flood said.

"No," Mr. Miller whispered.

"You could use something."

"I know, I know," Mr. Miller answered. "I want to stay awake."

Mr. Flood eased himself onto the bed next to Mr. Miller. He took several Kleenexes from the night table and gave them to Mr. Miller. "You done?" Mr. Flood asked. He held the tissues under Mr. Miller's nose as if he were waiting for him to sneeze. Slowly Mr. Miller put the pan down on the bed and took the tissues. He put them to his eyes and then put his left hand out and said, "More." Mr. Flood handed him the box. He took a handful and buried his face in it. He cleaned his nose and mouth and then looked down into the lump of soggy tissues and said, "That jackass thinks God is an accountant."

"Sure," Mr. Flood said.

"There isn't any God, Flood, just Christians."

"I know," Mr. Flood said.

"Don't pacify me," Mr. Miller said, but before he could gather enough breath to go on another coughing spasm hit him.

"You're getting awfully sick," Mr. Flood said.

"Shut up," Mr. Miller hissed.

Mr. Flood patted Mr. Miller's back several more times as he coughed, but it did no good. Mr. Miller dropped his hands into his lap and let his chest relax. It bumped up and down as if it were operating independently of the rest of his body. He sat there all curved over staring at the floor, his chest working but producing no fluids at all. He dry-coughed for about five minutes, each spasm slightly weaker than the one before it, and he stared down in a desolate gray way as if the floor were an ash heap.

Only Mr. Flood looked up when the front end of a large metal cart pushed its nose into the room. When one of its wheels caught on the door it backed up and then shot into the room, pulling a woman behind it. It was clear that her red and white striped uniform had been made with a much younger person in mind. It was very tight through the chest, and the space between the hem and the knees laid bare four and a half inches of thighs that were heavily weather-beaten. Mr. Flood watched her as she took a miniature clipboard from the metal cart and checked it carefully. With the eraser end of a giant toy pencil pointing at the two men she said, "Mr. Flood or Mr. Miller?"

"What do you want?" Mr. Flood asked.

"I'm Doris," she said. She tapped a nameplate that protruded from her left breast. "Now, Mr. Miller first," she said. She stepped around the cart and approached the two men. As she did Mr. Miller raised his head slightly to look at

her, but then he coughed again and looked back to the floor.
"What do you want?" Mr. Flood said again.
"Why, to give you things," she said. "From the Auxiliary." She gestured back to the cart.
"Why?" Mr. Flood said.
The woman looked bewildered for a few moments and then she said proudly, "I'm a volunteer."
"Please go away," Mr. Flood said to her. She pivoted quickly and went back to the cart. She began taking small items and putting them in a clear plastic bag that had a large red heart on it. First she put in a toothbrush, along with a sample-size tube of toothpaste, then a ten-cent comb and a small bottle of after-shave that looked like a complimentary cocktail on an airplane. Finally she took a booklet from the top of a large pile and wedged it next to the toothbrush. She closed the top of the package and took two steps toward Mr. Flood and Mr. Miller. She handed the package to Mr. Flood and then went back to the cart and started to fill a second one. Mr. Flood held the plastic bag up and looked into it. He read the title on the booklet through the plastic, *Our Heart's with You*. Underneath it in smaller type was written, "Get Well Soon!"

When the woman was finished with the second package and was sealing it up, Mr. Flood said to her, "You get out of here, lady." She turned to look at him and it was clear that she was suddenly afraid. "Get out, I said," Mr. Flood repeated.

"What's the matter?" She held the plastic bag in front of her like a purse.

"You got until I count three," Mr. Flood said.

"I don't understand."

"And then I'm going to break your goddamn neck."

She put the plastic bag down quickly on the foot of Mr. Flood's bed and grabbed the end of the cart. She tugged it into the hall, turned it just outside the doorway and wheeled it away as fast as she could.

Mr. Flood turned his full attention to Mr. Miller, who had slumped very slightly toward him. "I got to get somebody

Going Gently

for you," he said. Mr. Miller raised a hand and indicated again that he did not want anyone else. "I never seen you looking like this," he said to Mr. Miller.

"I'm going to be all right," Mr. Miller said. "It's just a low point. No arms, no legs."

Mr. Flood helped Mr. Miller ease back onto the bed, and then he took the small metal pan and set it on the night table. Mr. Miller looked up at him.

"Do you want yours?" Mr. Flood asked. He held up the little plastic bag.

"No," Mr. Miller answered. Mr. Flood leaned over and dropped the bag into the wastebasket just under the head of the bed. Next he took the wad of Kleenexes and put it on top of the bag. "I've got it a lot worse than you, Flood," Mr. Miller said. "I'm way ahead of you."

"Sure," Mr. Flood said.

"I *am* sicker," Mr. Miller insisted.

"Good for you."

"I don't need anybody," Mr. Miller said. His eyelids fluttered as he fought to keep conscious.

"So who does?" Mr. Flood said. He shuffled back to his bed slowly and leaned against it with his hands, like a drunk against a building. He steadied himself for a few moments, and then he saw the other plastic bag at the foot of his bed. He straightened up, reached for it and looked briefly at its contents. Then he threw it into the hall.

The next morning the doctors drained Mr. Miller's right side and this time he could not sit up by himself. Miss Scarli supported him from one side, an orderly held his right arm down and forward from the other side. The doctors were quick and efficient with the procedure and it went off without a word being spoken. When Miss Scarli gathered the soiled instruments together after they had drained him, she stood and looked at Mr. Miller for a long moment. It looked as if she were going to speak to him but she didn't. She went to Mr. Flood's bed with the doctors, and as they gave him a routine examination he stared out between the two men, his once round, jolly face now saggy and pointed at the chin. "How long?" Mr. Flood said without looking at them. When they did not answer he repeated himself and cocked his head to one side waiting for an answer. The doctors finished their work and left him without even the barest indication that they had heard his question. "Pretty soon," Miss Scarli said to him.

"A couple of days?"

"Three, maybe four," she said. "I don't know."

"Mr. Miller said a week," he told her without looking up.

"He hasn't got that," she said.

"He's going to go before me," Mr. Flood said. His face looked as if he had just discovered a horror. "I don't want that," Miss Scarli looked at him intensely. "He's such a goddamn windbag," Mr. Flood said. Then, after a moment, "What will they do to him when he dies?"

"Is it so important?"

"I want to know."

"The procedure is to secure the wrists and ankles with gauze," she said with great formality. "Then they put a diaper on you and two orderlies put you on a cart and take you downstairs."

"What happens there?"

She shifted her weight uncomfortably. "They put you in the 'fridge until your funeral director comes and takes you away."

"It ain't no big deal."

"I wouldn't think too much about it if I were you," she said.

"It don't make any difference," he said. "I ain't real depressed any more." There was no quality to his voice. "I'm way on the other side of being depressed."

She pulled the things in her arms closer to her and stepped back from the bed. "Will you be all right?" she said.

He looked at her and then at Mr. Miller. "Sure," he said.

Miss Scarli left the room and Mr. Flood sat looking at the lump that was Mr. Miller. "You crumb bum," he said to him. Mr. Miller stirred a little on his bed and Mr. Flood knew he

Going Gently

was trying to turn over to face him but had no strength. Mr. Flood watched Mr. Miller's shoulders move, then his knees and feet. But there was no follow-through to the movements, and they became almost frantic as Mr. Miller tried several more times to gain the leverage that would get him over. When he was finally able to turn and lie flat on his back his breathing was very fast and light. "For all your big-deal facts, Mr. Miller, you don't know what they do to you after you're dead."

"That's of no importance," Mr. Miller answered. His voice was barely a whisper.

"How do you like the idea that they're going to put a diaper on you?"

Mr. Miller's head moved very slightly, and with effort his eyes caught Mr. Flood's.

"A diaper?"

"A diaper."

Mr. Miller looked away and thought for a moment. "Logical," he said. "I have never considered it, but it is highly logical."

"Maybe to you," Mr. Flood said. He looked to the floor.

"You see, Flood, at death the autonomic nervous system . . ."

"Shove it."

At that moment Miss Scarli returned carrying a large envelope in front of her as if it were a tray. "Here," she said to Mr. Flood. "There's a man outside who says he's your lawyer." He looked at the envelope and then up to Miss Scarli. "Here," she said again and offered him the envelope. He took it and put it across his knees. "You're supposed to sign each original and each copy in the spaces indicated," she told him. She stood patiently while Mr. Flood took the papers out of the envelope and began to sign them. He was quick and efficient and when he was done he put them back in the envelope and gave it to Miss Scarli. After she had left the room Mr. Miller said to Mr. Flood, "What were the papers?"

"Christ, I don't know."

Going Gently

That afternoon things were not good. Just after lunch, which neither man ate, Mr. Flood spontaneously lost control of his gut. He lay in bed with his legs moving in slow circular motions as if he were on an invisible bicycle. Mr. Miller lay on his left side watching Mr. Flood, but he was unable to raise his arm to ring for Miss Scarli. He drifted in and out of consciousness, and each time he closed his eye he gripped the edge of the mattress as if to ensure that when he awakened he would still be in the same position. It was not until the orderly came with the juices just before four o'clock that Mr. Flood's condition was found out. And even then it took nearly twenty minutes for Miss Scarli and two nurses' aides to get to the room. They went to work on Mr. Flood with their usual efficiency, rolling him first to the wall, then back, and just as they completed their work Mr. Flood vomited gray gastric juices onto the mattress and down to the floor. "Damn you," Miss Scarli said, but Mr. Flood did not hear her. One of the aides asked Miss Scarli if they were to change the sheets again. Miss Scarli looked at her watch and said that the evening shift could do it.

As she turned from Mr. Flood's bed she looked at Mr. Miller. He was still on his left side and there was a soft sleepy smile on his face. Miss Scarli stood there until the aides had left with the bundle of soiled sheets and then she stepped closer to Mr. Miller. "What are you smiling about?" she said.

"I'm coming out of this one," he said very quietly.

"You sure?" She leaned down very close to him.

"All over the feelings are familiar."

"You're beating some pretty good odds," she said.

"I'm glad you left Flood's sheets," he said.

"It doesn't make any difference."

"I know," Mr. Miller said. He looked at her for a long time as if he were going to ask her something, but he did not. Finally she told him she had to go and give report to the evening staff. "What will you do when you get home?" Mr. Miller asked.

"Feed my cats," she answered.
"How many?"
"Two."
"Then what?"
"I'm not going to do this, Homer," she said. "I'm not telling you anything more about me." She started to back away from the bed. "I've got to give report," she said, and she was gone from the room.

Mr. Miller rolled slightly onto his left side and looked over to Mr. Flood. He called his name softly twice, but there was no answer. Mr. Flood looked gray and dead, and for just an instant Mr. Miller thought he was. He called again, and this time Mr. Flood twitched a little in response. Mr. Miller tried to sit up in bed, but his efforts were meaningless. He tried to half-roll over and reach for the book on his night table, but he never even got close. Finally, his breathing coming very lightly, he lay back again on the bed and looked at the window. He stared out at the sky, which was just beginning to dim down into an early winter sunset. The colors that ran along the few clouds in the distance were weak and faint. Yet there was a kind of radiation in the pinks and oranges that rimmed the clouds, a kind of glow that lingered on their edges and seemed somehow to spread beyond the clouds to the air itself. Mr. Miller watched the colors dilute over the next few minutes and then dissipate toward the horizon in long gray streaks, as if the sun were drawing all the light from the sky back into itself. Then, abruptly, it was long past sunset and the light in the room flattened out along the walls and floor, and then even the shadows were finally gone.

Mr. Flood was not conscious long enough that evening to have his dinner fed to him. It sat forty minutes on the big sliding bed table in the middle of the room. Mr. Miller, though, ate very well with the help of a young orderly he had never seen. The young man propped Mr. Miller in bed very carefully and fed him patiently. Quite suddenly during the meal the young man looked toward Mr. Flood and then back to Mr.

Going Gently

Miller. "How do you think he is?" he asked. He watched Mr. Miller's face very carefully.

"More soup," Mr. Miller said.

"You think he'll be all right for a couple more days?"

"Who knows?" Mr. Miller opened his mouth and eagerly took in a spoonful of soup.

"One of the interns said he won't last the night."

"Don't you worry about Flood," Mr. Miller said.

The young man continued to feed Mr. Miller, and between mouthfuls he turned and looked at Mr. Flood. Mr. Miller concentrated on his food with obvious delight, and he became angry when the orderly did not feed him fast enough. But during the middle of the meal Mr. Miller suddenly became very tired and told the orderly he was finished. As the young man removed the tray Mr. Miller asked him to roll down his bed. There was a certain frantic quality to Mr. Miller's voice, as though if he were not flat in the next few seconds he might lose control of himself and tumble helplessly out of bed. The orderly rolled down the bed and gathered the utensils and put them on the tray. As he started from the room he stopped at Mr. Flood's bed and carefully studied him.

As he left the room Mrs. Marvin came in to take Mr. Flood's blood pressure. A stethoscope hung from around her neck to her groin and she carried the blood-pressure cuff in her hand as if it were an old baseball glove. She glanced at Mr. Miller and then went to work on Mr. Flood. She took several readings, the last two very carefully, and removed the cuff. "Is he all right?" Mr. Miller asked in a whisper.

"He's doing surprisingly well," she answered.

As she began to roll up the cuff Mr. Miller said, "Aren't you going to do me?"

"There aren't any bets on you," she said.

Mr. Miller turned his head slightly and said, "How many in the pool?"

"Everybody."

"Scarli?"

"No, not Miss Scarli," she answered.

Going Gently

Mrs. Marvin finished rolling up the cuff and took the stethoscope from around her neck. As she turned to leave the room she said, "The pool's worth thirty dollars."

Mr. Miller awakened the next morning to see Mr. Flood sitting on his bed with his robe around his shoulders. Mr. Miller quickly propped himself on his elbow and said, "What the hell are you doing?"

"I woke up a couple of hours ago," Mr. Flood said. "I felt like sitting up."

"Don't you feel sick?"

"No, not now."

"Have you been out of bed?"

"I ain't Superman."

At that moment Miss Scarli came into the room like a whirlwind on legs. At first she looked very angry, but when she saw Mr. Flood sitting up she seemed to calm down. She looked first at him, and then at Mr. Miller, who raised a hand from the bed. Mr. Flood sat looking at the floor, and it took him several seconds to notice Miss Scarli. "What are you doing sitting up?" she asked. There was true amazement in her voice.

"A guy can sit up if he wants," he said. He glanced at Mr. Miller.

"Are you all right?" she asked.

"Flood's all right," Mr. Miller answered for him.

She went to Mr. Flood and stood in front of him, blocking his view of Mr. Miller. "Is there anything I can get you?" she asked.

"Pea soup," Mr. Flood said flatly.

"I mean medication," she said.

"Just pea soup," he said, "a great big bowl of it."

"I'll see," she said. "It's seven-thirty in the morning, you know."

"Thick," he said. "Like you could eat it with a fork. And two pieces of rye bread."

"You want to lie back?"

"I'm okay," he answered. He raised a hand slightly and Miss Scarli backed away from him. She watched him looked down to the floor, and then his eyes traveled over it to the wall. He cocked his head in a strange way, as if he were listening for something, and then he stared back again at the floor.

Miss Scarli stepped very close to Mr. Miller and bent down to him. She put her hands on the mattress and held herself there as if she were in the middle of a push-up. "You know about the pool, don't you?" she said.

"There could be nothing in this world more insignificant," he said. She started to raise herself up and Mr. Miller looked at her very directly. "Kiss me," he said.

"Never," she said. She smiled warmly as she stood erect. She turned away from Mr. Miller to see that Mr. Flood had eased himself back on the bed and was trying to get under the sheets like an animal going to its hole. She went to him and helped him turn around. He sat half-propped against the head of the bed and he said, "The soup. I really want the soup."

"Yes, yes," she said and left the room.

"What is this sudden fetish for pea soup, peddler?" Mr. Miller said. Mr. Flood did not appear to hear him. He lay in the bed with the sheet up to his chest, his arms lying hard by his sides. He did not move except to lift both hands a little way off the bed and slowly turn them over and look at them. The expression on his face seemed to say that he did not believe the hands were his.

Mr. Miller got into a sitting position with great effort. He sat on the edge of the bed with his legs jutting out like a child sitting in a chair far too big for him. He eased forward until he was able to dangle his legs straight to the floor. They were chalk white and there was no more hair on them. "Jesus," Mr. Flood said very softly. He dragged the word out as if it were a whole sentence. "I'm scared as hell," he said.

"See here, Flood," Mr. Miller said.

Mr. Flood half-turned toward the middle of the room. "I don't never want to go through that again," he said. "Never."

"Make sense, peddler," Mr. Miller said.

Going Gently

"This morning, between five and seven," he said. "I don't never want to be that lonely again."

The orderly came in carrying a small tray with the pea soup on it. He stood like a stranger in the middle of the room and said, "Who gets this?"

Mr. Miller told him to put it on the bed table in the middle of the room, and he began to struggle into his robe. The orderly set the pea soup down and left the room without looking at either man. Mr. Miller knotted the robe about his chest and slowly slid from the bed. He stood for several long moments leaning against the mattress. Finally he took two shaky steps and put both hands on the bed table. Using it for support he rolled it toward Mr. Flood's bed. It slid around Mr. Flood like a giant clamp. Mr. Miller leaned heavily on the table with his elbows as he took the metal food warmer off the bowl of soup. His arm operated like a little crane. "Why pea soup?" he asked. Mr. Flood did not answer. He only opened his mouth like a baby and waited while Mr. Miller stirred the soup and then put a spoonful to his own lips. "A little hot," he said, but then he reached out and fed Mr. Flood the remainder of the spoonful. Mr. Flood took it in as though it would give him life. "They didn't send the rye bread," Mr. Miller said. Mr. Flood only opened his mouth more.

In a few minutes the soup was gone and Mr. Miller stood watching Mr. Flood's mouth play with the after taste. "Thanks," Mr. Flood said after a few moments. His eyes set themselves on Mr. Miller. "It's all right now," he said in a sudden burst of energy. A little color flushed along his cheekbones.

"You know, Flood," Mr. Miller said, "this is a false world."

"Knock it off," Mr. Flood said quietly.

"That is not intended to be a pessimistic observation," Mr. Miller said.

"Knock it off," Mr. Flood said with a little smile.

Mr. Miller eased back from the bed, pulling the table with him. He turned and guided it toward his own bed, and it was clear that he could not have gotten there without it. He half-fell, half-rolled into his bed and lay there for a very long time looking at the ceiling. When he gathered all his strength and turned to look at Mr. Flood he saw that he was again unconscious. Mr. Miller rolled to his back and with a delicate gesture pulled the sheet to his chest, and almost immediately he was asleep.

Mr. Miller did not awaken until very late afternoon, and when he did he rolled again to his left side and called, "Flood? Are you there?" He waited as long as he could for an answer, but none came. In a few minutes he lost consciousness.

Mr. Flood died the next morning after a nice winter sun had come up. Miss Scarli put the time at seven-fifteen. Mr. Miller went into a coma shortly afterwards, and he died during the afternoon of the following day. No one was sure of the exact time.

About the Author

ROBERT C.S. DOWNS has published five novels and has had one screenplay produced by CBS. NBC, CBS and the BBC have made television movies of three of his novels. A graduate of Harvard and the University of Iowa Writers' Workshop, he has taught at the University of Arizona and now lives in State College, PA, where he is Professor of English at Penn State. He is married and has two daughters. He has been a Guggenheim Fellow, and has received an NAACP Image Award.

Photo by Susan L. Downs